THEFT

Riverfront Books and Stationery in the Roberts Building, 1117 Commercial, Astoria. Wednesday, $6000 in office equipment and software inventory was stolen when intruders broke through the basement door, Astoria police said. Owner Georgia Madison was called to the scene. Also on hand was Ben Stratton, new owner of the Roberts Building.

⚞ FAMILY ⚟

1. **HOUSEBOUND—**
   Anne Stuart
2. **MOONLIGHT AND LACE—**
   Linda Turner
3. **MOTHER KNOWS BEST—**
   Barbara Bretton
4. **THE BABY BARGAIN—**
   Dallas Schulze
5. **A FINE ARRANGEMENT—**
   Helen R. Myers
6. **WHERE THERE'S A WILL—**
   Day Leclaire
7. **BEYOND SUMMER—**
   Karen Young
8. **MOTHER FOR HIRE—**
   Marie Ferrarella
9. **OBSESSION—**
   Lisa Jackson
10. **TRUST A HERO—**
    Muriel Jensen
11. **GAUNTLET RUN—**
    Joan Elliott Pickart
12. **WEDNESDAY'S CHILD—**
    Leigh Michaels
13. **FREE SPIRITS—**
    Linda Randall Wisdom
14. **CUPID CONNECTION—**
    Leandra Logan
15. **SLOW LARKIN'S REVENGE—**
    Christine Rimmer
16. **UNHEAVENLY ANGEL—**
    Annette Broadrick
17. **THE LIGHTS OF HOME—**
    Marilyn Pappano
18. **JOEY'S FATHER—**
    Elizabeth August
19. **CHANGE OF LIFE—**
    Judith Arnold
20. **BOUND FOR BLISS—**
    Kristine Rolofson
21. **IN FROM THE RAIN—**
    Gina Wilkins
22. **LOVE ME AGAIN—**
    Ann Major
23. **ON THE WHISPERING WIND—**
    Nikki Benjamin
24. **A PERFECT PAIR—**
    Karen Toller Whittenburg
25. **THE MARINER'S BRIDE—**
    Bronwyn Williams
26. **NO WALLS BETWEEN US—**
    Naomi Horton
27. **STRINGS—**
    Muriel Jensen
28. **BLINDMAN'S BLUFF—**
    Lass Small
29. **ANOTHER CHANCE AT HEAVEN—**
    Elda Minger
30. **JOURNEY'S END—**
    Bobby Hutchinson
31. **TANGLED WEB—**
    Cathy Gillen Thacker
32. **DOUBLE TROUBLE—**
    Barbara Boswell
33. **GOOD TIME MAN—**
    Emilie Richards
34. **DONE TO PERFECTION—**
    Stella Bagwell
35. **POWDER RIVER REUNION—**
    Myrna Temte
36. **A CORNER OF HEAVEN—**
    Theresa Michaels
37. **TOGETHER AGAIN—**
    Ruth Jean Dale
38. **PRINCE OF DELIGHTS—**
    Renee Roszel
39. **'TIL THERE WAS YOU—**
    Kathleen Eagle
40. **OUT ON A LIMB—**
    Victoria Pade
41. **SHILOH'S PROMISE—**
    BJ James
42. **A SEASON FOR HOMECOMING—**
    Laurie Paige
43. **THE FLAMING—**
    Pat Tracy
44. **DREAM CHASERS—**
    Anne McAllister
45. **ALL THAT GLITTERS—**
    Kristine Rolofson
46. **SUGAR HILL—**
    Beverly Barton
47. **FANTASY MAN—**
    Paula Detmer Riggs
48. **KEEPING CHRISTMAS—**
    Marisa Carroll
49. **JUST LIKE OLD TIMES—**
    Jennifer Greene
50. **A WARRIOR'S HEART—**
    Margaret Moore

FAMILY

Muriel JENSEN

Trust a Hero

DESPERATELY SEEKING DADDY

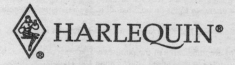

HARLEQUIN®

TORONTO • NEW YORK • LONDON
AMSTERDAM • PARIS • SYDNEY • HAMBURG
STOCKHOLM • ATHENS • TOKYO • MILAN • MADRID
PRAGUE • WARSAW • BUDAPEST • AUCKLAND

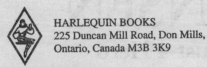

HARLEQUIN BOOKS
225 Duncan Mill Road, Don Mills,
Ontario, Canada M3B 3K9

ISBN 0-373-82158-1

TRUST A HERO

Copyright © 1990 by Muriel Jensen

This edition published by arrangement with Harlequin Books S.A.

® and TM are trademarks of the publisher. Trademarks indicated with
® are registered in the United States Patent and Trademark Office, the
Canadian Trade Marks Office and in other countries.

Look us up on-line at: http://www.romance.net

Printed in U.S.A.

Dear Reader,

Trust a Hero was born in the wee hours of a cold December morning when I was called by the police to the bookstore I managed in downtown Astoria. There'd been a robbery and the basement door had been ripped off its hinges.

Astoria is built over the rubble of a fire that destroyed much of the town in the 1930s. The result is a downtown that sits over a warren of tunnels that lead into many of our commercial area's basements. Burglaries are a major nuisance—particularly at 2:00 a.m.

That particular morning, as I rehung the basement door, I entertained myself by plotting a romantic mystery involving the tunnels and the heroic owner of a bookstore and her handsome new landlord. That's the best part about writing for a living— everything, even being dragged out of your warm bed at 2:00 a.m.—is story material.

It was also a comfort to me that my imagination and my sense of humor could still function at that hour! I hope you enjoy the result.

Muriel Jensen

To Amy Wetherill Baker
and Julie Wetherill,
who inspired Linda and Lacey

CHAPTER ONE

BEN STRATTON FLIPPED ON the light switch and walked cautiously down the old wooden basement stairs. He was pleased to note that they felt solid under his feet. He glanced around as he descended and saw a bare bulb hanging on a chain, shelves neatly stocked with supplies and an orderly stack of unopened cartons against the concrete wall. Hundred-pound sacks of flour and sugar lay on pallets several inches off the floor. The owner of the Astoria Bakery was a tidy tenant—not very friendly, but tidy.

Ben walked across the scrupulously swept floor, seeing cracks in the concrete that had been laid more than sixty years before. He frowned. This close to the river there would be water seeping up when it rained.

He flicked on the flashlight he held and directed the light at a dark corner. There were cracks in the wall, too, but they were small, and he saw no evidence of dampness or the fine powder in the cracks that indicated current movement. Odds and ends of lumber were propped up against the wall. Moving to the opposite corner, he swept the light up a delivery shoot to inspect the underside of the double metal doors that opened onto the sidewalk in front of the building. He heard conversation and footsteps clanging on the doors as people walked by overhead.

Methodically, he swept the flashlight from beam to

beam. They appeared sound. There was no evidence of dry rot or any of the many insect infestations that could reduce wood to chips. It appeared David had made a good move when he purchased the Roberts Building.

"You doing all right down there?" A female voice called from the top of the bakery steps.

"Fine, thank you, Mrs. Hansen," he replied, grinning to himself at the owner's perfunctorily polite tone. He was sure she had concluded the moment he'd introduced himself as one of the new owners of the building that he planned to raise the rent or evict her or both. "I won't be much longer. I just want to have a look at Mrs. Madison's side of the basement."

"The light switch is at the top of her stairs." The door slammed, punctuating her brusque advice.

And they say people in small towns are friendly, he thought wryly. Moving out of the circle of light, Ben wandered slowly into the dark half of the basement that belonged to Riverfront Books and Stationery, picking his way carefully in the beam of his flashlight. His foot collided with something hard and solid, and he swept the light drown, finding a sea of cartons, invoices still attached. He smiled again. Obviously not as tidy a tenant as Mrs. Hansen. Winding his way through the boxes he found the stairs and climbed them, then flipped on the switch.

He looked at his watch: 8:35 a.m. He'd better get the lead out if he wanted to finish this tour before the other shop opened. He knew the Roberts Building's other tenant already considered her new landlords intruders in her life. He didn't want to contribute to her annoyance and natural suspicions by being around when it was time for her to open for business.

GEORGIA MADISON WALKED down Commercial Street toward the bookstore, humming to herself. It was a rare, sunny April morning and her long-awaited stock had arrived just the day before. It had been almost three months since the sale of the building in which she was a tenant, and the new landlord hadn't been heard from. Her fear of an exorbitant rent increase or eviction had begun to die down. Added to that was the extra bonus of finding on sale the very sweater that Lacey wanted for her birthday. Life was good.

Remembering the white cotton dress for herself she'd seen while shopping for the sweater, Georgia summoned her willpower and walked past the bakery without stopping for her customary blueberry muffin and coffee. Glancing in the window as she passed, she caught sight of Karen Hansen at her cash register and waved. Her short, plump neighbor smiled and waved back.

Georgia stopped in front of the double glass doors of Riverfront Books and Stationery and fit her key into the lock. Mentally, she listed everything she had to do today. Check in yesterday's freight, wrap Lacey's sweater, sign the birthday card, pick up the cake from Karen and water Bea's plants. Smiling wryly, she considered that modern woman's greatest freedom was the right to decide *which* eighteen hours to work in order to make time for everything she had to do.

Georgia pushed her way into the shop, then turned and locked the door behind her. Leaving the lights off, she dropped her purse on the counter and took a moment to look around her shop in satisfaction. After two years, the fact of her proprietorship still filled her with pride and a very elemental thrill she admitted was probably unsophisticated. The store satisfied a personal need that hadn't been necessary when Gary was alive, and a very practical need when his untimely death left her and the girls without support.

She breathed in the smells of paper, wood and ink, the perfume of her financial independence. It was true that loans from her mother-in-law and the bank had helped make it possible, but she was paying the money back as promised and on time. In all the years she had worked beside her husband, keeping the books for the freight business that had been in his family for three generations, she'd been included in his plans and helped make decisions. But planning, deciding and implementing her own had provided a thrill she hadn't expected.

"Speaking of implementing..." she told herself aloud, heading for the basement stairs. If she didn't get busy with yesterday's freight, she wouldn't have it checked in and brought upstairs before it was time to open the store.

The sudden strip of light visible beneath the basement door alerted her. When she'd put her hand on the knob an instant ago, it had been dark. There was a sound on the stairs on the other side of the door, and her heart rose to her throat.

Then anger and resentment filled her as she remembered all the inventory she'd lost and the frustration she'd suffered at the hands of this thief. She also remembered what she'd heard at the police department's special seminar for merchants on dealing with the sudden wave of thefts downtown. "If you arrive at a robbery in progress," the officer had cautioned, "do not attempt to stop the thief yourself. Go to the nearest phone and call the police." She promptly pushed the advice to the back of her mind.

When she'd been robbed the month before last, the thief had taken her adding machine, her tape player and a whole case of her most expensive pens. Last month he'd taken her new adding machine, her new tape player and several cartons of computer software she'd been waiting for for four months. She was beyond being reasonable or cautious.

Certain the thief was some punk kid supporting bad habits by selling the inventories of the merchants on Commercial Street who worked hard for *their* money, Georgia decided to act. Quietly turning the knob, she pushed the door back suddenly with the full force of her 118 pounds. The door struck something solid, from which she heard a satisfyingly startled grunt, then there was the sound of something clattering down the stairs. She reached around the door, grabbed a fistful of what felt like flannel and yanked. "Come out of there you little parasitic menace to society!" she shouted, and with her free hand, grabbed the long-handled tool propped against the wall near the door. As she continued to yank, the perpetrator, encumbered by surprise and the steps, stumbled around the door and up into the store.

Georgia shoved him against the wall, then held the tool against his chest, her weight behind it, to hold him there. "I want to know what you were doing in my basement," she demanded in a hard voice, applying a little more pressure before he entertained any thoughts of trying to break away. He looked at her with startled hazel eyes, and she glowered back at him, realizing for the first time since she'd heard the noise that she'd done a truly stupid thing. This thief was not the youth she had imagined.

He was a man. A big man. In worn jeans and a blue-

and-gray flannel shirt with the sleeves rolled up, he appeared to have a good ten inches and probably seventy pounds on her. His light brown hair was tousled and dusty, and now that the initial surprise of her attack had passed, he did not look pleased. Georgia recalled that the police suspected the recent rash of burglaries was being coordinated by someone and was not the usual hit-and-run tactics of rowdy kids.

Fear began to dilute courage. It was a long way to the phone, the front door was locked, and she was holding a seasoned thief at bay with a window squeegee. With forced bravado, she asked again, "What were you doing in my basement?"

Ben tried hard to engage his sense of humor. When he thought about it, being pinned against the wall by a dark-haired woman half his size wielding a large windshield wiper was funny—as long as none of the guys he played tennis with found out about it. But he'd gotten up at five to drive up from Portland to look over the building Dave had purchased in the interest of making improvements. The owner of the bakery had been openly hostile, but this woman was making her look like a paragon of graciousness. There had to be humor here, but he couldn't quite bring it into focus.

"I'm here," he said with quiet care, "to make certain the building is structurally sound."

"Ha!" Georgia said. "You must think I'm structurally defective, if you expect me to believe that."

Ben looked at her short, dark hair, parted on the side and just skimming her chin in a loose wave, down the trim, subtly rounded lines of a lavender suit, along elegantly shaped calves to small feet in black, wedge-heeled shoes. His gaze went back to wide brown eyes that were now watching him with less anger than caution. "Hardly," he replied.

Apparently alarmed by his scrutiny, she applied more pressure to the squeegee. "Look, you..." she began to threaten.

"Mrs. Madison." He took a firm grip on the end of the handle closest to him and pulled it out of her hands without too much effort. "Now that you've rearranged my ribs, let's talk about this like civilized people." He propped the squeegee against the wall with a decisive thud and rested his hands on his hips. "I'm your landlord."

If he'd expected that news to change her attitude, he was mistaken. He was suddenly facing the business end of a pair of long-handled tongs, a device probably as old as the building. Its ends were sharp.

"I've met the man who bought the building," she said, beginning to look nervous despite her bravado. "You're not him."

Ben closed his eyes, summoning patience. "That was my uncle, David Wilson. He buys and I restore. We're partners."

She studied him a long moment, but she didn't drop the tongs. Taking them away from her, he decided, would require more skill than the squeegee.

"Oh, yeah?" she said finally. "Let's see your driver's license."

Instinctively, he put a hand to his back pocket. It was flat. "It's in my jacket," he said, watching the suspicion that had begun to recede in her eyes blossom again.

"And where's your jacket?"

"At the bakery."

"Sure."

Enough was enough. Ben grabbed at the handle, careful to reach beyond the nasty-looking points. But she was expecting the move this time and danced backward, jabbing him. He stopped, a long red gash on his forearm.

Ben bit back an expletive and studied the wound. It was nothing more than a good scratch, but it made him think twice about trying that again. "Mrs. Madison," he said wearily, "you're beginning to annoy me. You pay five hundred dollars a month rent, you haven't had a lease for the last two years, the building's furnace was on the fritz for the entire month of January, and you and Mrs. Hansen have had a running battle with the old landlord for a year and a half to repaint. Would a thief know all that?"

Oh, God. How else would he know that? Georgia's determination wavered, but she continued to keep him at a distance. "That sounds convincing, but I'm not entirely sure I believe you."

"Believe him." Karen Hansen suddenly appeared from the basement steps, wiping her hands on the apron that covered her baker's whites. She looked from her friend to her new landlord, obviously trying to decide why Georgia was holding the tongs on him and why he was bleeding. "I went downstairs to get a carton of napkins and heard the commotion. You threatened to raise the rent?" she asked Ben.

He folded his arms. "I had hoped to be finished before Mrs. Madison arrived, but she came in earlier than I expected, heard me in the basement and mistook me for a thief."

Karen burst into laughter, then stopped immediately, making a brave effort to look sober when no one joined her. "He is our new landlord, Georgia," she said, taking the tongs away from her friend. "Mr. Stratton, this is Georgia Madison, owner of Riverfront Books and Stationery—privately, a serial killer whose weapon is a pair of antique tongs."

Georgia glanced darkly at Karen, then looked into the hazel eyes she'd been confronting for the past five minutes, hoping to see a glimpse of humor there. It was minuscule, but she found it. He crossed the distance that separated them and extended his hand. The fact that the arm that connected it to his body was now bleeding made her groan as she took it.

"Hi," she said feebly, pulling him by the hand across the room to the bathroom beside her office. "Let me wash that off for you. I...suppose I can expect an eviction notice in the morning." She glanced at him with a cautious smile as the two of them crowded into the tiny room. Karen stopped in the doorway, folded her arms and leaned against the molding.

Georgia turned on the cold water and eased Ben's arm under it. He had to lean down to cooperate, putting them eye-to-eye across the sink. His hazel eyes studied her with new interest, and she looked away, concentrating on washing his arm.

"It's just a scratch," he said. "Worth a little more rent, maybe, but hardly eviction."

"You'll have to forgive her," Karen said from the doorway. "Her store's been robbed during the night four times in the last year, three times within the last four months."

Georgia turned the water off and reached to the rack for one of the fluffy towels she'd brought from home. She dabbed at his arm with it, then rested his elbow on it as she rummaged in the medicine cabinet over the sink for antiseptic.

Ben straightened, offering his arm when Georgia un-
capped a bottle of iodine. "Mrs. Hansen let me into
her basement to check for structural problems. Obviously we want to take care of those before doing the
cosmetic work the building needs so badly. Since you
share the same basement, I didn't think you'd mind me
checking your side while I was down there. I went up
the steps just to put the light on. I wouldn't have let
myself into the store without your permission."

Now convinced he was innocent of thievery, Georgia
looked him in the eye. His gaze was direct. She liked
that; she was very straightforward herself. "So, what
are you going to do with the building, Mr. Stratton?
Rumor has it you and your uncle have office buildings
up and down the Oregon coast."

"Rumor is right," he said.

"Is that what you plan for our building?"

Her contrition seemed to be giving way to a suspicion she'd probably held since Dave had bought the
building. Ben was relieved that the tongs were out of
reach. "We have no specific plans at this point, except
to be sure the building is safe."

Georgia spread antiseptic liberally up and down the
gash. The scratch wasn't deep, except for a small spot
near the inside of his elbow, but she suspected that it
stung furiously. Still, he didn't react. "You have two
fiscally sound, responsible tenants right now, Mr. Stratton."

"He could divide the building into four smaller offices," Karen pointed out coolly, "give the building a
face-lift and get a lot more rent."

Georgia tore the wrapper off a bandage and placed
it over the deeper edge of the wound. The forearm she
worked on was long, well muscled and tan. Obviously

a wheeler-dealer type, she thought, with time to go to a gym and vacation in the sun—like the men who ruined Gary. Her task completed, she folded her arms and looked up at him. "Is that the plan?"

The atmosphere in the tiny bathroom was now thick with hostility; Ben felt it surround him. His tenants had obviously decided he was not to be trusted. That made him hostile, too.

He looked into Georgia's eyes, unsmiling, as he rolled down his shirtsleeves. "I just said we didn't have a specific plan."

Georgia and Karen looked past his shoulder at each other. He had little trouble reading the isn't-this-just-what-we-expected look on their faces.

"We're to believe," Georgia asked, "that a high-rolling buy-up team from Portland bought a decrepit old building in the boonies with the intention of leaving it as it is?"

Buttoning a cuff, Ben looked down at her with all the disdain she showed him. "Of course not," he said. "You could believe that we simply wanted an investment here, a good reason to weekend at the coast. You could believe that we want to be sure this old building is safe for you, and that we'd like to make it as attractive as possible so that it will be appealing to the tourists you depend on so that you and then we can make a profit. But small-town folks are always convinced that big-city people are out to take advantage of them. I wouldn't want you to buck a trend."

Never one to be unfair, at least not knowingly, Georgia had the grace to look ashamed. "Was that your plan?"

When he reacted with an impatient roll of his eyes, she added quickly, "I know. So far you don't have a plan. But if you did, might it include letting us stay here?''

He gave her a smile she didn't trust. "Half an hour ago, it did. Since then I've had a doorknob driven into my stomach, a squeegee into my ribs and sharp tongs into a main artery. Right now I'd cheerfully rent your spot out to rotating rummage sales.... If I can have fifteen more minutes in your basement, I'll be on my way."

Wordlessly, Georgia swept a hand toward the basement. Karen stepped aside to let him through the doorway. She and Georgia looked at each other as his footsteps sounded across the back room, then grew faint as he went down the basement stairs.

Karen walked into the bathroom to slap Georgia's arm. "Good work, Georgie. I've always wanted to peddle my wares out of a cardboard box in my golden years with you for company."

Georgia frowned at her. "You're the one who suggested he was going to change the building into an office complex."

"But I didn't leave the mark of Zorro on him, then suggest he was a liar."

Georgia's shoulders sagged. "If we had any chance of staying here in the beginning, I've probably blown it."

Karen put an arm around her. "Phil says not to worry about it until we know we have to leave."

"Your husband carries a gun. He doesn't have to worry about things. If people don't do what he wants, he can throw them in jail or shoot them."

Karen looked at Georgia. "He insists that being a police officer is more complicated than that. Now come on, cheer up." Karen drew Georgia out of the bathroom toward the shop. "Let me out the front door and I'll bring you back a blueberry muffin and a cup of coffee and you'll feel better."

"I'm trying to diet. There's this white cotton dress at Leon's—"

Karen interrupted. "I don't want to hear about it. I never wear anything white after hours or anything I have to diet to get into. And, anyway, how can you be dieting? Aren't you taking the girls for pizza tonight for Lacey's birthday?"

Georgia nodded, turning the lock on the front door. "I'm sure I'll burn off the calories maintaining order among four teenage girls."

"Your mother-in-law going?"

Georgia shook her head. "Bea's still in Cozumel with the senior citizens' tour. She'll be back in a couple of days."

Karen smirked. "Then there's a chance you'll have fun tonight."

Georgia swatted her friend's arm scoldingly. "Bea's a good-hearted lady. She's just..."

"Bossy."

"Yes. But if it hadn't been for her, I wouldn't have the store." Georgia sighed, then hugged her friend. "Thanks for coming to check on me. If you see Mr. Stratton again, tell him..."

"I'll tell him you have lapses of sanity." Karen opened the door, letting in a gust of cool morning air. It smelled of cedar and sun and the river a block away. Entwined in it were the wonderful aromas from Karen's bakery. "Actually, he's gorgeous for a land-lord, isn't he?"

Georgia lifted a shoulder. "He's big. I didn't really notice that he was gorgeous."

Karen shook her head over Georgia's indifference. "Will you wake up? Gary's been gone over two years now, Georgia. It's time you started noticing men."

"Karen…" Georgia began.

"I know, I know. You and the girls are doing fine on your own, and the circumstances of Gary's death make it hard for you to… I mean…" Cornered by her own concern, Karen looked up at Georgia, wondering if she'd said too much.

Georgia made a conscious effort not to stiffen. Karen meant no harm. "When I'm ready for a relationship," she said quietly, "I'm capable of looking for one. I really am. So don't worry."

Karen took her hand and patted it. "I know you are, but Phil and I are worried about you. The longer you remain withdrawn—"

"I'm not withdrawn, I'm busy," Georgia said. Taking another whiff of the air from the bakery, she smiled at Karen. "Oh, what the heck. If you have time, bring me a muffin and coffee."

Karen gave her a look that told her she knew she'd been deliberately diverted and went off with a wave. Georgia left the door open, flipped the Closed sign to Open and turned on the lights, appreciating what a close call that had been. She'd almost had to talk about Gary's death.

After taking the cash drawer out of the safe and putting it in the register, she went to the long display window, pulling a few books out to make room for new stock. Glancing up, she saw Ben Stratton walk out of the bakery, shrugging into a light cotton jacket. He got into a red Chevrolet four-wheel-drive pickup and drove away.

Talk about close calls, she thought, watching the

truck turn down Twelfth Street. She had almost am-
putated her new landlord's arm. She could always
move to the shopping center. So the rent was twice
what she paid; the foot traffic was supposed to be twice
what they got downtown. But she didn't want to be in
the shopping center. She wanted to be here, where
she'd started, where she could see and smell the river,
feed the pigeons, kibitz with all the friends she'd made
on Commercial Street.

There was no alternative, she realized as she dropped
a stack of books on the counter. Somehow, she'd have
to straighten things out with Ben Stratton.

CHAPTER TWO

"NO MUSHROOMS!"

"Mushrooms are good! There aren't any calories in mushrooms."

"Could we *please* have one half with anchovies this time? I mean, it is my birthday."

"Anchovies? Yuk!"

"Wait, wait!" Seated at one end of the table occupied by her two daughters, Linda and Lacey, and Lacey's two best friends, Georgia raised both hands to try to reestablish order. The noise level in Mr. Fultano's was such that she had to shout to be heard. "Let's try to get together on this. Are there any two of you who want the same thing?"

The four girls in jeans and purple-and-gold Astoria High School sweatshirts stared back at her without response. Georgia was forced to admit that *had* been a silly question. She tried again. "Who wants the vegetarian *with* mushrooms?"

Linda, small and curvaceous at sixteen, raised her hand. She counted every calorie religiously, including the ones she was sure were in toothpaste.

"Without mushrooms?"

Lacey's friend Kristin raised her hand, round spectacles and retainer winking under the overhead light.

"And anchovies for Lacey. What about you, Dina?"

The tallest of the group, Dina was shy and stoop

shouldered from trying to hide her awkward height among her shorter friends. "Taco pizza, please, " she said.

"Okay." The choices memorized, Georgia stood. "Save the table, and I'll place our order. Diet Pepsi all around?" That, at least, was unanimous.

Georgia went to the counter and gave her order to a tall, redheaded young man. She dug a pen out of the bottom of her purse and opened her checkbook, then drew a mortified breath as she stared at the deposit slips that were all that was left in it.

The young man, who had just rung up her twenty-seven-dollar order, looked at her warily. "Changed your mind?"

"No, I'm out of checks," she groaned, routing through her billfold and coming up with $5.41. Then inspiration struck. "Is Mr. Fulton working tonight?" She served on a merchants' association committee with Robert Fulton. She was sure he'd extend her credit until the following day.

"It's his night off." The boy calmly dashed all her hopes, reminding mercilessly, "It's $27.50, ma'am. Shall I cancel the order?"

Behind her a group of obviously hungry young women in bowling uniforms fidgeted. Georgia turned to the table of giggling girls and groaned to herself. She would just have to drive home and back....

"Place the order." A long arm shot past her shoulder, a lean hand passing two bills to the relieved cashier.

Georgia spun around in surprise, finding herself nose to nose, or rather, nose to clavicle with her landlord. "Mr. Stratton." She felt caught between pleasure and embarrassment. His willingness to help her suggested he wasn't holding a grudge about that morning, and she had hoped for an opportunity to apologize for it. But it would probably have helped her case if she'd projected an image of competence and control; forgetting her checks hadn't done that. "Thanks, but I can't let you—"

"Please," he said. "I'd like to."

"Really, I..."

"I insist."

"Two large pizzas," the cashier repeated to Georgia, apparently considering it wise to make sure she hadn't changed her mind now that the man had appeared. "One half veggie with mushroom, one half without. One half veggie with anchovies, half taco. And a pitcher of Diet Pepsi."

She nodded, then turned back to Ben, planning to thank him. She opened her mouth, then closed it again when he held her to him as he reached over her shoulder to accept his change. He smelled of the leather of his jacket, she noticed, and a crisp, woodsy after-shave. It was the lightest touch of his hand at her back, a slight, brief flattening of her breasts against his chest, but her heart gave a formidable lurch. A reaction to surprise, she thought, ruffled but trying to appear calm as they moved along the counter to the clerk who would provide their drinks.

"Either you're very hungry," Ben said, "or you're not here alone."

She pointed across the room to where the four girls were huddled together, giggling. "It's my youngest daughter's birthday. Four growing girls can get very hungry."

Daughters, Ben thought, looking down at her ringless hands on the counter. He turned to the table and saw that the girls made a beautiful picture, like something an Impressionist might have painted: two pale, curly heads together with a brunette and a redhead, eyes flashing, bubbling genuine laughter—emerging femininity at its most touching. He felt a sudden ache for all he'd missed as a child, for all he was missing now. "The dark-haired one's yours," he guessed.

"And the redhead. She's the birthday girl, Lacey. the other is Linda."

Ben turned back to Georgia, letting his eyes wander quickly over her jeans and red sweater. He found it easy to forgive her for that morning. "I would never have taken you for the mother of two teenagers."

The boy behind the counter poured Diet Pepsi into a frosty pitcher. "I wouldn't have figured you for a landlord," she said, then laughed when his mouth took on a wry twist. "I guess I made that obvious."

The boy put the filled pitcher on a tray and pushed it toward Ben. "Your number is thirty-nine. Thank you."

Before Georgia could reach for the tray, Ben pulled it off the counter. "I'll carry this to the table for you, then leave you to your party."

As they approached the table, Georgia saw her daughters staring openmouthed at Ben Stratton.

"Girls," she said brightly, suddenly unaccountably nervous. "I'd like you to meet one of the new owners of the Roberts Building." The girls stared. "Mr. Stratton, these are my daughters, Linda and Lacey, and Lacey's friends, Kristin and Dina."

Ben put the tray in the middle of the table, smiling at the girls as he did so. "Good evening, ladies. Happy birthday, Lacey."

Lacey stood and offered her hand. "Thank you. Happy to meet you, Mr. Stratton."

"Ben," he corrected.

Georgia often prayed that her younger daughter would acquire a little subtlety to temper the honesty and enthusiasm with which she greeted life and everyone in it. But at the moment, her unqualified warmth and eagerness to talk covered her mother's nervousness. It also prevented Ben from leaving as he'd promised. She pulled up an extra chair. "Mom says you're going to make smaller offices out of the building and throw everybody out on their duffs."

Georgia folded her arms on the table and dropped her head on them. She heard Ben's light chuckle as Lacey went on. "You wouldn't really do that, would you? Mom's a widow and she works without anyone to help her so she can save money. It'd cost her a bundle to move. Are you married?"

Trying desperately to maintain a grip on the conversation but losing, Ben replied, "No, are you?"

The girls laughed. "No." Lacey rested her chin on her hand. "I'm not going to get married. I'm going to be a veterinarian and live alone on a big farm. But there is *someone* at this table who isn't married, either."

Linda rolled her eyes. "None of us is married," she said impatiently, "and you're embarrassing Mom. Right, Mom?"

Mortified, Georgia glanced at their guest and couldn't help laughing. "Yes. And probably Mr. Stratton, too."

He looked more amused than embarrassed. "I'm a bachelor and I like it that way," he said, filling the girls' glasses from the frosty pitcher. "And pretty as your mom is, I'm sure she's single because she wants to be."

Kristin, who was the youngest of seven children, looked surprised. "But, don't you want to have kids?"

"Oh, sure," he said, pushing a filled glass her way. "But my work keeps me going from place to place a lot. When you do that, it's hard to find a wife. And if you don't have a wife, you can't have children."

Tensely expecting one or all of the girls to take him literally and correct him on that, Georgia was pleasantly surprised when he added smoothly, "Of course, you *can*, but that's not good for anybody. Georgia?"

"What?" Her name on his lips, so easily spoken, startled her.

He gestured with the pitcher. "Pepsi?"

"Oh, yes." Realizing she was clutching her glass, she held it out for him to fill.

Lacey frowned. "I thought a landlord stayed around to watch his property. Why do you go from place to place?"

"Because my uncle and I own quite a few buildings on the West Coast. I travel around to all of them to check on problems and see that the buildings stay in good repair."

Linda, a dedicated homebody, asked, "Don't you get tired of that? Don't you ever want to just stay in one place?"

Georgia saw the slightest flicker in his eyes when he considered the question a moment. Then he shook his head, smiling. "When I do, I have a condominium in Portland."

"Number thirty-nine," a disembodied voice called over the loudspeaker.

"That's us!" Lacey was on her feet in an instant to

accompany Ben to the counter. They were back in a moment, deep in conversation about the merits of anchovies. With both pizzas in the middle of the table, Georgia began distributing napkins while Ben refilled soft drink glasses. Then he leaned over the back of Georgia's chair and smiled at the girls. "Thanks for letting me crash your birthday party, Lacey. I've got to be on my way."

All the girls looked disappointed, but Lacey, who loved or hated people instantly, grimaced. "Can't you stay? You can share my anchovies."

Georgia noticed that the look of regret on Ben's face also seemed genuine. "Thanks, Lacey, but I have to go. Happy birthday."

"Maybe we'll see you at the store sometime," Linda suggested.

He smiled. "Maybe. Meanwhile, take good care of your mom."

Linda shrugged as though she had assumed that demanding burden long ago. "I always do."

Georgia pushed her chair back. "I'll walk you out. Be back in a minute, girls."

Ben pulled her chair the rest of the way out and guided her to the door with a hand on her elbow. The weather had changed, and a light rain was falling. They stopped just outside the door in the shelter of the portico. The dark parking lot seemed suddenly still and strangely intimate.

"I want to repay you for the pizza," Georgia said. Her voice was a little breathy, and she cleared her throat. "Shall I just put it in with the rent, or will you be around tomorrow?"

He shook his head. "Please don't worry—"

"Now I'm insisting," Georgia said. "If you hadn't

been here tonight, I'd have had to go all the way home for my checks. The girls might have expired of starvation. And—'' she drew in a breath, squaring her shoulders ''—I wanted an opportunity to apologize for this morning.''

She had to have the softest brown eyes he'd ever seen, Ben thought. And the prettiest mouth—pink and supple and... He put aside his thoughts, realizing she was expecting a response to her apology. ''It's not necessary,'' he said, zipping up his jacket. ''I'm sure a woman alone, particularly one who's been robbed so often, has to be careful.''

''I didn't mean that,'' Georgia admitted with a wince. ''I meant...suggesting you lied about what you planned to do with the building. Not that you have any plans, but if you did...'' Having effectively stammered herself out on a limb, she stopped. ''Do you have any idea what I'm trying to say?''

He laughed softly. ''I think so. Where did Lacey get the red hair?''

Surprised by the question, she hesitated a moment. ''Her father,'' she replied.

Ben saw a glimpse of emotion in her eyes—loss, he guessed, but something else...a pain that didn't seem to be a part of grief.

''He could also talk himself into or out of anything,'' she said dryly. ''She's very frank and brave. Heroic qualities, but sometimes they make polite conversation difficult.''

He laughed. ''She's charming—they both are. Will you be at the Downtown something-or-other meeting in the morning?''

Her eyes widened in surprise. ''The Downtown Enrichment Association. Yes. How did you know about it?''

''I checked in at the Chamber of Commerce to pick up a map and a few brochures, and the manager invited me to sit in and learn what's happening in Astoria. That's a fanciful name for a group of merchants.''

Georgia nodded with a wry smile. ''We were a little tongue-in-cheek when we voted on it. The group is composed of some downtown businesses who think historical enrichment and preservation will 'enrich' our cash registers as well as our city. It's a fun group of people.''

''I'll look forward to meeting them. We can haggle about the pizza then.''

''All right.'' Georgia nodded, pleased with the way this encounter had turned out. He could still decide to evict them and make an office complex out of the building, but at least it wouldn't be her fault. ''Meeting's at seven at the Red Lion.''

He smiled. ''That's where I'm staying. See you then.'' With a brief wave he loped across the parking lot to the red truck.

''HE'S CUTE, MOM.'' Linda sat at the kitchen table with a cup of cocoa. She wore a white flannel nightshirt with Garfield in nap-attack mode on the chest. Her long dark hair had been brushed until it shone—a nightly ritual.

Beside her, Lacey, in an identical nightshirt, rested her chin in her cupped hands, her cocoa ignored. Her brown eyes were dreamy. ''He's a little old, but cute.''

''He's not old,'' Linda admonished. ''At least, not too old for Mom.''

Across the table from the girls, Georgia sipped her coffee, afraid to examine that remark too closely. It was late and she should send the girls to bed, but she relished these few moments of quiet they shared before retiring. Their lives were already getting busy with school activities and phone calls and overnights with friends. In a few years, they'd have lives of their own that would involve her only peripherally.

"Don't you think he's cute, Mom?" Lacey persisted.

Georgia put her cup down. "No," she said, then could not stop the smile that came as her daughters watched her expectantly. "I think he's gorgeous."

"All right!" Linda slapped the table in excitement, and Lacey leaned forward enthusiastically. "Do you like him? He seems so great!"

"Actually, I don't know him that well." Georgia suddenly felt the need to dampen their fervor. Their intense interest in her remarrying was something they all teased each other about. She didn't mind it because it meant they were getting over the loss of their father, but as a serious consideration, it was out of the question. "He'll be coming and going like he said at dinner. He enjoys being a bachelor, remember?"

Lacey, who always heard and remembered everything, corrected her. "That's not exactly what he said, Mom. He said he'd like to have kids, but it was hard to find a wife when you moved around a lot. He seemed to like being with us tonight."

"And with you, Mom," Linda said seriously. "He kept looking at your hair."

Georgia felt a blush start at her neck and fought it off by collecting their cups. Was that true? she wondered. "You're making something out of nothing. He's just a good-looking man who bought the Roberts Building."

A silence fell over them as Georgia rinsed out the cups. Then Linda, wiping off the table, looked at Georgia over her shoulder. "Do you want to get married again, Mom?"

Georgia gave the faucet a sharp turn and reached for a towel. "I don't know." She turned to face her daughter. "Don't you think it's kind of fun, just us girls?"

"Yeah," Linda admitted, her tone conditional. "Except when the dishwasher breaks down or it thunders or—" she sighed, rinsing the sponge under the faucet "—it comes times for the Senior Class Father/Daughter Tea. I know I don't have to worry about it until next year, but I won't have a father then, either."

Lacey came to put her arms around Georgia. She felt fragile in the nightshirt, and Georgia held her close. "Why did Daddy have to die?"

The girls had grieved over the loss of their father, but they have never whined. Despite the complete shock of the accident and the ugly days before and after the funeral, they had gone back to their obligations at school and around the house with a courage that had inspired Georgia to go on. Otherwise, after what she had learned, she might have given up.

"Because," she said gently, philosophically, "things happen to us in life that we can't explain and can't do anything about, except deal with them as gracefully as we can."

"That's crummy," Lacey said feelingly.

Georgia rubbed her back. "That's life."

Lacey pulled back to ask, "Do you miss him?"

Georgia nodded, tears blocking her throat when she had thought she'd cried them all long ago. Her grief had been entangled in the mysterious circumstances of his death and the ugly things they implied. Still, she could recall so clearly how completely they'd loved each other, how happy they'd been, how much he'd loved the girls and Bea. Her memories could negate every grim implication of the way he'd been found—yet, it had happened.

"Always," she admitted. "But I just collect my good memories and think about them—even let them hurt a little—and I feel better." That wasn't precisely true, but it sounded reasonable and she wanted her daughter to feel at peace.

"It doesn't really hurt anymore," Lacey explained. "It's just that...when I get to thinking about it...it's like..." Uncharacteristically at a loss for words, she looked to her sister for help.

"Like something's missing," Linda provided. "Something important."

Georgia pulled Linda into her free arm and hugged her. "I know. When it comes time for the tea, I'm sure Mr. Hansen or Ragnar will be happy to escort you."

Linda nodded. "That's nice, Mom. It'd just be better if it was my own dad, you know?"

"I know, sweetie, but we have reality to deal with here." Georgia hugged her again.

Linda nodded grimly, then looked Georgia in the eye with a burgeoning smile. "Reality is that half the kids' real fathers won't be there. Heather Berger will probably have to go with her grandpa, Jill Warner goes everywhere with Misty Henderson and her dad, and poor Shelly will have to go with that old guy her mom's going out with. If she hasn't traded him in for somebody else by then."

"He isn't old," Georgia corrected, struggling with a laugh. "He's just bald."

"He's weird," Linda insisted. "He talks about money markets and CBs and stuff."

Wondering what citizens band radios had to do with careful investing, Georgia suggested, "CDs?"

"Whatever. He has Shelly putting thirty percent of her allowance into the stock of some computer company in Connecticut."

"When she could be buying *clothes*?" Lacey was horrified.

"Anyway," Linda said with a sigh, "I guess I'd be lucky to have Mr. Hansen or Rags to go with."

"Can we have leftover pizza for breakfast?" Lacey asked as Georgia led them up the stairs to the bedrooms.

"No, but you can take it with you for lunch."

"Don't forget to sign my permission slip for the field trip," Linda reminded. "I left it on the refrigerator."

"Right."

"And pick up my drill team skirt from the cleaners," Lacey said.

"Right."

"Thanks for the party, Mom." In front of her bedroom door, Lacey turned to give Georgia a hug. "And for the great sweater. I'm going to wear it to school tomorrow."

"Good," Georgia said, hugging Linda. "Then at the end of the week I can pick *it* up from the cleaners, too."

Giggling, Lacey disappeared into her room. Linda hesitated a moment, looking in concern at Georgia from the shadows of the hallway. "Are you going to be okay, Mom?"

Surprised by the question, Georgia smiled, wondering if her mother-in-control facade had somehow slipped. "Of course, Lindy. Why do you ask?"

Linda shrugged, leaning back against the door frame to her bedroom. "I don't know. I never thought about it much before, but tonight, when we saw Ben with you, I realized that you must get very lonely without Dad. It's been two years now, and you never go out with anybody."

Touched that Linda had thought along those lines, Georgia felt the strange tension that had plagued her all day soften. "Well, at my age you have other things to worry about."

"But men are important to a woman's life."

The bold statement was made with such conviction that Georgia felt an instant's panic over just what had brought her daughter to that conclusion.

"I mean..." Not usually at ease with baring her soul, Linda folded her arms and looked down at her shoes, then up at Georgia. "I haven't ever been in love or anything..." Georgia let her breath out slowly. "But I've worked with a lot of boys at school on the student council and with that fund-raising thing last year for the band. Most of them don't even see me. But there's this one boy..." Linda shrugged and blushed. "Well... he makes me feel special...pretty."

Georgia's maternal antennae rose. "Why don't you invite him over?"

Linda shook her head. "It's nothing like that. I don't think he really likes me—he's just nice to me."

"I promise I wouldn't mention marriage," Georgia teased.

Linda giggled and rolled her eyes. "I just meant that when he smiles at me, I feel like there's a glow here." She put a hand to her stomach, alternately smiling and frowning as though her thoughts confused her. "But there're lots of pretty girls after him."

"Honey, you're pretty enough to compete," Georgia said firmly. "You have so many fine—"

"Mom." Linda stopped her with mild impatience. "You think I'm special 'cause you're my mother. But the truth is, I'm just not very pretty and kind of... weird."

"Linda!" Georgia put her hands on her daughter's shoulders and shook her gently, alarmed by how near she stood to the brink of womanhood and by how sincerely she believed herself to be ordinary when, in truth, she was such a special person. "You're not *weird*. You're genuine. You never pretend to be someone you're not. And as far as not being pretty, haven't you looked in the mirror?"

Linda sighed and rolled her eyes again. Vaguely, Georgia remembered looking in the mirror at that age and being convinced that an ugly, large-nosed freak looked back at her.

"That settles it, then," Georgia said, giving Linda a hug. "I can't get married again. I have to look after my little troll. Or, who knows? Maybe one day love will sneak up on both of us."

Linda pulled away, giving her a scolding glance. "This is the nineties, Mom. A woman goes after what she wants."

Georgia pinched Linda's chin. "Then maybe you'd better take your own advice. Good night."

She went back to the kitchen to sign Linda's permission slip and replace it under the magnet so that she would remember it in the morning. During the nightly ritual of checking the burners on the stove, the coffeepot, and window and door locks, Georgia let herself think about Ben Stratton and the thoughts he'd inspired in Linda.

Linda was wrong, of course. A man wasn't important to Georgia's life at the moment. Financially, she was doing fine; as a parent, she had a blessedly good relationship with the girls; and as a woman...well, as a woman she'd been alternately stunned, hurt, defensive, stubbornly loyal and completely confused since Gary's death. Until she had some answers—and the likelihood of that happening was negligible—she couldn't embark on another relationship. She had to know what had happened to the one she'd had.

Not that Ben Stratton would ever see her as Linda thought he saw her, anyway. She groaned softly to herself as she flipped off the lights and climbed the stairs. She had accused him of being a "parasitic menace to society," threatened him with bodily harm, then slashed him with a pair of tongs. She couldn't help the smile that formed when she thought about that. Hardly inspiration for romance.

Georgia went into her bedroom, stopping on the threshold as she'd done every night since the day Gary died. She wondered if this feeling of being a stranger in her own room would ever change. Without her husband it seemed to lose all familiarity to her. The shades of blue and cream with which she had so lovingly decorated it several years ago now reminded her of something someone had tried to recreate from a picture in a magazine, somehow losing the warmth and personality that had been intended.

Loneliness swept over her, harsh and very real. She knew how to deal with it, but for a moment she didn't have the energy. It was such a solitary struggle, and it seemed to go on so long.

Then she remembered Linda reminding her that
"This is the nineties, Mom. A woman goes after what
she wants." Pulling off her clothes and changing into
a long, pink flannel nightgown, she had little problem
mentally listing what took precedence in her life. She
wanted her girls to be happy, well educated and on
their way to promising futures. She wanted Bea to
marry Rags and be happy, and she wanted to keep her
shop—in its present location—and see it prosper.

She set the alarm on her clock radio and climbed
into the middle of the cold bed, feeling better. It always
helped, she thought practically, to know your priorities.
It never occurred to her that she'd left herself out of
them.

CHAPTER THREE

"GEORGIA! HERE!"

Breathless, Georgia stopped her headlong rush into the Red Lion's banquet room and turned her head toward the sound of the voice. Karen waved at her from across a room that was filled with most of the membership of the Downtown Enrichment Association. Georgia waved back, forcing her way through the group just as the association's president banged his gavel.

"You missed breakfast again," Karen said with a shake of her head, pouring coffee for Georgia as she settled into a chair beside her and dropped her purse on the floor. "What crisis befell the Madisons this morning?"

"Don't be smug," Georgia scolded with a smile, eagerly bringing the cup of coffee to her lips. "Someday, if you and Phil decide to have children, you'll know what it's like, particularly if they're girls. They can't find their shoes, the right blouse isn't pressed, their hair isn't right. It's hard to be anywhere on time. Did you save me anything to eat?"

Karen reached behind the coffeepot to something wrapped in a napkin and handed it to Georgia with a grin. "What are friends for?"

"All right!" Georgia unwrapped a fat bran muffin and dropped it onto the empty plate before her, putting the napkin in her lap. "If I had an orange juice, life would be good."

A tall, slender glass of juice suddenly appeared in front of her, deposited near her coffee cup by a large male hand. She followed the white cuff and the gray wool sleeve over her shoulder to the now familiar face of Ben Stratton.

"Thank you," she said in surprise as he took the chair opposite Karen. "That was thoughtful."

In a crisp white shirt, subtle tie and three-piece suit, he looked very different from the the dusty, carelessly dressed man she'd mistaken for a thief yesterday morning. His brandy-blond hair was combed back into order, an apparently stubborn side part taking over anyway, the strands it disturbed beginning to curl. His hazel eyes were bright, more gold than brown in the sunlight coming in through the wall of windows that looked out on the river. He smiled easily at her. "I'd like to take credit, but Karen knew you'd be wanting it. I just went to the buffet table to get it."

"Well, thank you both," she said, giving each a wry lift of her eyebrow as she privately wondered why she should suddenly feel breathless. "I've come to a sorry state when my best friend and my landlord can second-guess my needs."

Ben frowned. "Why a sorry state? Why not consider yourself lucky?"

Karen refilled Ben's coffee cup, then her own. "Because Georgia prides herself on always being on top of things. And if it wasn't for a propensity for tardiness, she would be. Knowing someone's read her mind probably makes her feel vulnerable."

Georgia was saved from having to defend herself when the meeting was called to order. The association's president, Jasper Johnson, an attorney who'd been a friend of Georgia's family since she was a child, conducted the usual preliminaries. The minutes of the previous meeting were read, the treasurer's report given—bringing its usual groan—and various standing committees' reports presented, drawing everyone's halfhearted attention while breakfasts were finished and gossip was exchanged in whispers. Then Jasper called Georgia to the podium.

In surprise, Georgia looked at Karen. "Did he call me?" she whispered.

Karen nodded, also looking surprised.

"Why?"

"I don't know." Karen made a shooing motion with her hands. "Your request for a grant to buy the Jeremiah houses has probably offended the Paul Rotherman Foundation, and they're going to tar and feather you and ride you out on the old Burlington-Northern tracks. Go."

"Georgia. Please." Jasper's voice boomed through the microphone as he looked over the crowd, finally spotting Georgia as she stood and began to weave her way through the tables to the dais.

Ben watched the back of Georgia's white woolen dress as she made her way to the microphone. Glossy dark hair swung as she moved, slim hips swayed with unconscious grace, and long neat calves and trim ankles drew his eyes. She smiled at good-natured jibes from friends as she passed and swatted one older man on the shoulder when he caught her wrist and said something that made the rest of the table laugh.

It was easy to see that she was loved, Ben thought, though he'd had sufficient evidence of that while Karen clucked for half an hour before Georgia finally arrived.

He allowed himself a moment of wondering what that was like. He usually didn't indulge those kinds of thoughts because they led to other painful memories of a part of his life he liked to think was behind him. Still, he couldn't prevent a moment's jealousy, a stab of envy for the woman surrounded by the love and respect of people she'd known most of her life.

"She's a favorite around here," Karen whispered.

Ben looked at the faces turned fondly, expectantly, toward her and smiled dryly. "Hard to tell."

On the dais, Jasper put an arm around Georgia. Ben watched her fold her hands self-consciously, smile at the watchful group, then lower her eyes as the president began to speak. She looked touchingly vulnerable, something he'd have never suspected the previous morning when she was rearranging his ribs with a squeegee.

"I'm sure you all remember," Jasper said conversationally, "last fall when we thought it would be a good idea to help the Columbia River Pioneers Museum acquire the two houses owned by Hiram Jeremiah on Duane Street behind the Roberts Building." He looked over the group with the comfortable confidence of long acquaintance. "We knew that two preserved historic homes right downtown would be good for our businesses. Of course, none of us could afford to buy the houses, and the current owner, living in San Francisco, was unwilling to donate them. We all decided that applying for a grant from the Paul Rotherman Foundation was a great idea." He stopped to acknowledge more nods and more approving murmurs. "But none of us was willing to write up the application. We were too busy, or we didn't know what to say. We talked about hiring someone to do it but decided it should really be done by one of us, someone who'd grown up here and who could express what it means to us in a way that would get us the money. So Georgia volunteered to do it.'' Jasper gave her a paternal squeeze and smiled out at his audience. ''Well, guess what came to my home this morning by messenger?''

Ben heard Karen's intake of breath and saw Georgia's head snap up and turn to Jasper. She put both hands to her mouth and waited with the rest of the now silent group. But Japser's pause for dramatic effect was a moment too long. Georgia grabbed him by both lapels and demanded in a whisper heard by everyone, ''Did we get it?''

''We got it!'' he shouted.

Georgia screamed and wrapped her arms around his neck. The audience rose in a body to shout and applaud. Laughing, Karen kissed Ben's cheek, then ran to the next table to share the excitement with friends. Ben watched the pandemonium and wondered how many places were left in the country where this kind of camaraderie, this kind of common caring took place. Probably not many. People loved and cared about each other everywhere, but it had been his experience that people valued their independence and found it difficult to work together toward the same goal.

A burly young man in jeans and a dark sweater reached up to the dais to bracket Georgia's waist and swing her down. She was swept from table to table with hugs and handshakes. After five minutes, the president reconvened the meeting.

Karen came back to the table, quickly followed by Georgia, who was arm in arm with a precisely groomed dark-haired man no taller than she was. Ben noticed that the man took hold of her hand as he sat at a right angle to her, across from him. He glanced up at Ben, giving him a friendly smile, but his attention was all for Georgia even after the meeting resumed.

A hand went up at the table nearest the podium. "Are we going to delay work on the houses until after Columbia River Days at the end of May?"

Jasper turned his head toward Georgia's table. "Mesdames cochairmen?" He smiled and corrected himself, "Cochairpersons?"

Ben was surprised when all the women in the group laughed, unoffended by the little chauvinist joke.

Georgia looked at Karen. "You explain it," she said with a smile. "I'm resting on my laurels." At which remark the little man covered their joined hands with his other one. Ben could not quite isolate or identify the strange feeling of annoyance rising in him without apparent reason.

Karen stood, a fashionable blue jacket over her bakery whites. "I haven't seen Jasper's letter, but it was our understanding when Georgia applied for the grant that it would be at least six weeks after approval before we have a check in our hands, so I'm sure we won't be able to start on the houses for some time."

The subject of building contractors was discussed then shelved until bids could be obtained and discussed at a future meeting.

"Okay." Jasper consulted his notes. "Last order of business. We need a volunteer to coordinate the Columbia River Days Princess pageant with Knappa, Seaside and Astoria high schools."

A hand went up at the back of the room, and Jasper smiled. "Ah, Mrs. Butler. A winner of the pageant herself in 19...?"

The pretty matron at the back of the room called back, "Am I under oath?"

Everyone laughed and someone shouted, "The question should be, are you under warranty? All those teenage girls!"

"I can handle it," she boasted. Her approval was made unanimous by a round of applause, and the meeting was adjourned.

The small man across the table from Ben immediately took the opportunity to pull Georgia closer and kiss her cheek. "I can't believe you pulled it off! Remember how hard I tried to get us a grant two years ago and got nowhere? And I'm supposed to know how to do that stuff."

"Well, you should have asked me for advice," Georgia teased, turning to Ben, her cheeks flushed with modest pleasure in her success. "Mr. Stratton, I'd like you to meet Walter Bishop, curator of the Columbia River Pioneers Museum. Wally, this is Ben Stratton, the new owner of the Roberts Building."

Bishop stood, offering his hand, and Ben reciprocated.

"Do you believe this woman?" Bishop asked, his thin-featured face flushed with pride. "The grant will mean so much to us." He grinned at Georgia. "And who'd have thought it from the girl who ducked class to go to Young's River Falls with a quarterback."

"Come on, Wally." Karen took his arm and began to propel him toward the door through which everyone was crowding, hurrying to get to their cars to reach their shops and businesses in time to open. Georgia and Ben pressed in behind them.

Georgia looked up at Ben. "If you noticed the three old houses right behind our building, Wally owns the only one of the three that's painted. It once belonged to Godfrey Mitchell, an early river pilot here. The other two are the Jeremiah houses we were talking about.''

As the crush moved forward, Wally told Ben over his shoulder, "I still have years of work inside, but it's a wonderful house. Georgia and I fought over it, but I won.''

"Only because you had the cash deposit." Georgia grinned at him. "All I have are two kids who insist on eating and a voracious oil furnace.''

Nearing the door, Karen and Wally squeezed through an opening to their left just as a large man in front of Ben and Georgia swung a raincoat over his shoulders. Ben pulled her close, raising his hand in front of her face and ducking his head to cover hers as the thick, button-studded fabric flew at them. It slapped harmlessly against the side of Ben's head, and the man immediately turned to apologize. He was tall and thickly built. His contrition seemed to lessen when he saw whom he'd struck. He stopped beyond the door on the landing while everyone else rushed around them down the steps to the parking lot. Pale blue eyes looked at Georgia with animosity, and Ben put a hand on her shoulder, coming alert. Suddenly the warm, small-town atmosphere was shattered by the jarring note of the man's anger. He looked up at Ben in a moment of interest that contained no courtesy or even civility, then lowered his eyes to Georgia.

"So, the house hugger gets two more.''

Ben felt Georgia's shoulder stiffen under his hand. "It's a place of history, Rob. You can put your restaurant someplace else.''

"I wanted to put it on Duane Street. It was a good

commercial location and would have relieved us of two eyesores. You messed it up for me.''

Ben watched in admiration as Georgia smiled, making no effort to hide the fact she was pleased. "I know.''

The man bristled, glancing at Ben, then back at Georgia. "Good thing the cool widow's got herself a bodyguard. She might need him." He turned and hurried down the steps to a red Mercedes.

Georgia turned to Ben with a grin. "Thank you," she said. "If you hadn't been here, I think I'd have been fish food.''

He could see no real fear behind her brown eyes, but she looked just a little shaken. Ben retained his hold on her shoulder and started down the steps. The early sun had gone into hiding, and a sky now heavy with pewter clouds was spitting rain. "There seems to be one person in Astoria who doesn't love you. Where's your car?''

She pointed across the lot to the blue station wagon, and they started toward it. "Rob MacKay is always at odds with everybody. He wants to bring in a Super Steaks franchise, which is a great idea. But he wants to tear those old houses down to make room for it. Wally and I have been fighting him for a year.''

"Why didn't he snarl at Wally?''

They stopped at the station wagon, and Georgia leaned against the door to face him. She rubbed her wool-clad arms against a cool breeze coming off the river, then pointed to Wally and Karen, already at their cars. "Fortunately for Wally, he was out of the way. Actually, I offend Rob more because I'm a woman, I suppose. He hates to be outmaneuvered by anybody, but he dislikes me particularly." She shifted suddenly, putting her large leather purse on the front fender and routing through it. "About the pizza..."

"Forget it," he said. "You can take me for pizza when I come back to town."

She turned, a frown between her eyes. She replaced it immediately with a tentative smile. "You're leaving now?"

"I've got to get back. I'm supposed to be in Salem tomorrow." He looked at her seriously. "You watch out for that MacKay character. I don't like his looks or his attitude."

She dismissed him as a threat with a wave of her hand. "I've been arguing with him for years. Well—" she held a hand out to him "—it's been nice meeting you...." She laughed. "And I apologize again for yesterday morning."

He engulfed her small hand in his, not surprised to note that, despite its size, its shake was sturdy. "It's all right. It's nice to know someone's guarding the building."

"When will you be coming back?" she asked, then added casually, "I mean, you still have to decide what to do about it."

He smiled. "I know what I'd like to do," he said noncommittally, "but I have to discuss it with my uncle. I'll be back in a couple of weeks to have a tenants' meeting with you and Karen."

Georgia nodded, wishing he could offer a little more reassurance but understanding his position. She pulled her keys out of her purse and opened her car door. "We'll see you in a couple of weeks, then. Goodbye." In a matter of seconds, Georgia was in the car and heading east on West Marine Drive back to town.

Her hands were steady on the wheel, but something

deep inside her was trembling. Residual fear from that encounter with Rob MacKay? she wondered. Partly. But part of it was a disjointed memory of having her head pulled into Ben Stratton's shoulder. The left side of her face had rubbed against the roughness of nubby wool, while the right had been pressed into a warm hand. The smell of his woodsy after-shave was a fresh memory in her nostrils even now.

As her mind replayed the scene that had followed with Rob MacKay, she could feel the weight of Ben Stratton's hand on her shoulder.

God, she thought worriedly as she braked for a red light. *Have I been alone too long?*

"YOU WANT TO WHAT?" The voice at the other end of a perfect telephone connection shouted, as though something had interfered with his hearing.

"I'd like us to just give the building a new front and leave it as it is." Ben spoke from the sofa of his motel room, looking out the double glass doors to the fishing boats bobbing at anchor in Astoria's west mooring basin. In the darkness, light bloomed from several of the boats, and the rest were highlighted by the floodlights from the motel. It was a pretty sight that eased the tension he usually felt when he was on business. "It has two thriving tenants at the moment, and they've just gotten some kind of grant to restore a couple of old houses. They're really into preservation. I'd like to give the building a new front appropriate to the historic atmosphere here and wait on any major changes."

"Ben," his uncle said reasonably, "I always trust your judgment on these things, but we are in the business of acquiring and restoring to make a profit."

"We have a building you bought for a song. It's in

good repair, and for the price of a face-lift, we'll get steady rents. We can always subdivide later if I'm proven wrong.''

There was a moment's pause. ''You're sure?''

''Yes.''

''All right. Will you be back in the morning?''

''No, I thought I'd hang around a few days and talk to an architect, then bat his ideas around with a builder.'' Ben hesitated, waiting for David to protest. When he didn't, he added, ''You'd better send Kimball to Salem. I could be tied up for a few days.''

That did make David react. ''Ben, is there something you want to tell me?'' he asked.

Ben smiled to himself. He could imagine David, who liked detail in everything, pulling at his thin gray hair. ''You sent me to do a job,'' he replied easily. ''I'm just trying to do it right. If my staying is a problem, I can leave early in the morning and be in Salem before lunch.''

''No....'' David said uncertainly. ''You do what you have to do. I can send Kimball. Just keep in touch.''

''Don't I always?''

''When it suits you.'' David's reply was not so much a criticism as a statement of fact.

Ben smiled again. ''All right, Unc. I'll give you a call as soon as I know anything I can pass on.''

After bidding his uncle good-night, Ben hung up. Pushing the double glass doors open, he stepped out onto the small fenced-in area that separated the motel from the riverbank. He drew in a deep breath of air and was surprised to find nothing offensive in the smell of diesel and fish. Woven into it was the tang of evergreen, the sweetness of an early spring night and the mysterious fragrance of the river.

Leaning his hands on the wrought iron railing, Ben looked out at the boats and wondered why he was still here. All the things he told David he wanted to do, he could have done by phone. Something he couldn't quite define had made him stay.

Astoria was a pretty town filled with nice people. That was true, but Oregon was full of pretty towns and nice people. Ben straightened, folded his arms and acknowledged to himself that Astoria had Georgia Madison in it. He had a vague memory of silky hair that smelled of something sweet and herbal against his face when he'd shielded her from MacKay and his errant raincoat. The soft skin of her forehead had grazed his chin; her hand had made a startled movement to his chest and he'd felt the warmth of it through his shirt and undershirt. His hand went to the spot now, rubbing as though the feeling lingered. He remembered also a subtle look of disappointment in her eyes when she realized he was leaving.

You're a loner, he told himself severely. *You've never been loved, you don't know how to give love, you have no business looking for it.* Ben instantly denied to himself that he was looking for anything, except signs of structural problems in the Roberts Building. Following that thought was the mental image of a frightened but courageous Georgia holding him against the wall of her back room with a squeegee. He laughed into the darkness despite himself.

Turning back into the room, he closed and locked the doors, then drew the drapes. The trouble with the world, he'd often thought, was that people analyzed too much. They overlooked simple pleasures or successes or ruined them by picking them apart to determine why they were. He wasn't going to do that, he decided, heading determinedly toward the shower. He wanted to have another look at the building, maybe look up photos of old Astoria to get some ideas for the renovation. If he saw Georgia Madison again in the process, that would be a bonus. But he wasn't looking for anything.

"LAST CALL, LACEY!" Georgia shouted from the bottom of the stairs, pulling on a silky fuchsia raincoat. "One more minute and we leave without you!"

Linda, calm and organized, books in her arms, purse and gym bag hanging over her shoulder, said dryly, "She probably has an eyelash out of place."

"Or she rewashed her hair." Georgia checked her purse for apple and granola bar. "She thinks it'll dull the color."

Linda laughed without humor. "She wishes she had my color. Can you imagine? This—" Linda held a glossy, wavy strand of rich brown away from her head with disdain "—in place of that red?"

"Careful," Georgia cautioned. "Your hair is just like mine."

"It looks good on you because you're...mature," Linda explained diplomatically. "But the guys at school notice great bodies and great hair. Guys in my class are already looking at Lacey."

In the process of bustling Linda toward the door, Georgia stopped, sensing they'd bumped up against a sensitive subject. Though almost two years younger, Lacey was already three inches taller than Linda. Her graceful neck, ghostly slender torso and long limbs were giving every indication of developing into a spectacular body. Georgia suddenly wondered if that contributed to Linda's blurred self-image.

"Does that bother you?" she asked gently.

Linda looked up at her and gave her one of those smiles that told her she saw through the question to what her mother really wanted to know. "It doesn't make me hate her, if that's what you mean. Who could hate Lacey? But I am jealous." She sighed, watching as Lacey, looking like something out of *Seventeen* magazine in black jeans and a lavender-and-black sweater, appeared at the top of the stairs. "I take care of my clothes, put my makeup on carefully, do my hair, and I always feel pretty when I leave the bathroom. Then I run into Laccy and suddenly feel ugly."

Georgia took Linda's chin in her hand and looked down into her eyes. "Am I ugly?" she asked.

Knowing what she was getting at, Linda rolled her eyes, trying to pull away, but Georgia held fast. "Answer me," she said mildly. "Am I ugly?"

"No, Mom," Linda replied reluctantly, "you're not ugly."

"You'd even be pretty," Lacey, who had just come downstairs to join them, contributed enthusiastically, "if you'd take your hems up a little, tighten your—" She stopped midsentence when Georgia shot a quelling look at her.

Georgia turned her attention back to Linda. "Remember how your father always used to say you were cloned from me?"

Expecting that memory to cheer Linda, Georgia was surprised and dismayed when Linda's eyes filled with misery and her bottom lip gave an alarming quiver. Then Linda shook her head. "He probably didn't mean it," she said, and turned to walk out the door.

Georgia caught her arm and stopped her, surprised by Linda's reaction. "Why do you say that?" she asked.

Linda looked into her eyes for a moment, swallowing with obvious difficulty. She glanced at Lacey, then said with a sigh, "We're going to be late for first period, Mom."

Georgia worried about that exchange as she drove back to town from the high school. Linda's grief over her father had always seemed complicated by something else, something Georgia couldn't understand. She'd always attributed it to Linda's age. Adolescence was a time of such emotional upheaval that a serious loss was bound to hurt longer and require a slower return to normalcy.

Usually, Linda gave every indication of having recovered, but once in a while, like the other night and this morning, Georgia would glimpse something in her—some buried pain that had been ignored and was now ingrown. She was a good and dutiful child but much more private than Lacey, and Georgia tried to give her latitude there, tried not to force confidences she wasn't willing to share. But she might have to take a different tack here, she decided.

Parking her car in her usual spot, two blocks from her shop on a side street to leave the convenient parking for shoppers, Georgia walked briskly to Commercial. Maybe one day, she thought wryly, the Downtown Enrichment Association could do something about downtown parking.

Waiting for the light to change on Duane Street, she glanced to her right, where the two rickety old houses sat, and smiled with satisfaction. "You're going to live," she told them quietly. A well-dressed woman with a hat stopped beside her, glanced in the direction Georgia had been looking and saw no one to whom she might have been speaking. When Georgia smiled and said "Good morning," the woman gave her a quick, humoring smile and decided to cross in the other direction. Georgia laughed and walked on.

Running into the bakery, Georgia waved at Karen, who was busy transferring a sheet cake to a box, and ordered her usual muffin and coffee to go. In front of the bookstore, she balanced purse, bag and coffee to find her key and turn it in the lock. She had almost an hour to check in the stock she'd been meaning to get to for two days.

The door unlocked, she shouldered it open, then stopped two feet inside to gasp in shock and dismay. Her cash register was on the floor, every standing rack was on its side, and cards and notes were spewed all over. Half the books had been pulled off the shelves and strewn around, computer disks had been bent and tossed everywhere, and reams of paper had been torn and thrown like confetti. She put a hand to her pounding heart. Fear rose in her throat and she took several steps forward.

"Stop!"

CHAPTER FOUR

GEORGIA SPUN AROUND, backing away at the sound of a masculine voice. Relief washed over her when she recognized Ben. Forgetting that he was supposed to have left for Portland yesterday, she knew only that she was glad to see him. She went toward him, hands outstretched. "Somebody trashed my store," she said in a voice that was half hurt and half indignant.

Taking her hands, Ben pulled her out onto the sidewalk. "Go to the bakery and call the police," he said.

"No, I want to..." She tried to go past him, back into the shop. The store had become so much a part of her, she felt a need to walk through it, assess the damage, check the basement.

Ben stopped her with firm hands on her shoulders. "No," he said implacably. "Go call the police. I want to make sure there's no one inside."

She looked up at him stubbornly. "It's my shop," she said.

"It's my building," he returned quietly. "Go to the bakery, call the police, then wait out on the sidewalk." When she hesitated, he added, "Please, Georgia."

It had been two years since Georgia had had to bow to someone else's will, but she did it, however grudgingly.

Ben picked his way through the mess, heading for the back room and the basement stairs. Everything that could be overturned had been, and all stationery racks and shelves had had their contents thrown onto the floor. There was cruel and wanton destruction in the torn paper, ink splashed against the back wall and small pieces of office equipment that had obviously been thrown and stomped on.

Going cautiously down the basement steps, Ben found that the cartons he'd stepped over two days ago were intact, but the shelves had been overturned, contents strewn across the concrete floor. What could be broken had been.

Uneasiness began to grow inside him when he saw that the bakery's half of the basement was completely untouched. Any thought that this was a random act of vandalism was dashed by the orderliness across the room.

After a complete tour of the basement, Ben was satisfied that the perpetrators were no longer in the shop. He ran back up the stairs, stopping at the top at the sight of a green smock hanging on a hook in the back room. A knife had cut it into fringe. His feeling of uneasiness became full-blown fear for Georgia and an anger so fierce he had to concentrate on quelling it to think straight.

He went back across the littered floor to the sidewalk, where Georgia waited with Karen. Standing on the other side of Georgia was a stout, gray-haired woman with a ferocious frown and the air of a top sergeant with an intestinal disorder. The fact that she had a brightly colored piñata under one arm and a serape over her other shoulder contributed to Ben's confusion. Before he could say anything, the woman demanded, "Well, young man. Who do you think you are to keep us cooling our heels out here?"

Georgia smiled thinly at Ben. "Ben, I'd like you to meet my mother-in-law, Beatrice Madison. Bea, this is Karen's and my new landlord, Ben Stratton."

"Good morning, Mrs. Madison," Ben said. "Or should I say, ¿*Buenos días?*"

"Good morning," Bea replied without expression, apparently unimpressed with his attempt at humor. "I'd like to go in now and look around."

"We'll wait for the police," Ben said, smiling but firm. "They should be along in a minute."

"Young man," Bea said, squaring her impressive proportions. "This shop is my daughter-in-law's livelihood, and I have a financial investment in it, as well as an emotional investment in her. As you are merely passing through Astoria, making a little money off the locals as you go, I fail to see how that empowers you to keep me out of here."

Ben looked down into the woman's affronted blue eyes and ignored the insult to his absentee landlord status, striving for patience. Though he found her corseted body and Victorian demeanor a refreshing change from the Nike-clad, tennis-playing grandmothers who populated much of the West Coast, he recognized spoiled willfulness when he saw it and didn't mind exerting his own. "Your financial investment happens to be in my building," he said evenly, "and you and your emotional investment are safer out here until the police arrive. The floor is littered with junk you could easily turn an ankle on, and it would be best to leave everything undisturbed for the police. They might see something we wouldn't notice."

She glared at him mutinously, then, apparently giving the matter thought, had the grace to agree that he was right. "Very well," she said. She handed the piñata and the serape to Karen. "May I use your telephone to call Mr. Jyhla?"

Karen nodded. "Of course, Bea."

When her mother-in-law disappeared into the bakery, Georgia pulled her raincoat more tightly around her. "I'm sorry," she said. "Bea's used to having things her way. She's really a very kind person."

Karen looked up at him and shook her head. "No, she's not." Prepared for Georgia's predictable defense of the woman, Karen turned, forestalling her. But the appearance of a police car at the curb prevented an argument.

A tall officer with boyish good looks and a shorter, dark-featured man with the look of a seasoned veteran, though Ben guessed he wasn't yet forty, emerged from the car. As the young man peered inside the shop, Georgia introduced the veteran as Phil Hansen, Karen's husband.

"How far in did you go?" he asked Georgia.

"Ben went inside and down to the basement. He didn't see anyone."

The man gave Georgia's shoulders a squeeze, winked at Karen, then went in with his partner, gesturing for the others to follow. At the sight of the damage, Phil whistled and pushed his hat back on his head. "Stay near the counter," he advised, "until we look around."

"I'll get you some fresh coffee." Karen dropped Bea's gifts behind the counter and headed off to the bakery. She and Bea passed in the doorway.

"My God!" Bea exclaimed as she took several steps into the shop. She put an arm around Georgia and patted her stoutly. "You poor dear. Don't worry about a thing. I'll help you clean up and we'll find a way to replace your stock until your insurance comes through.''

"Thank you, Bea." Georgia hugged her. "But don't *you* worry. I can take care of things.'' She pointed her mother-in-law toward the chair behind the counter. "Phil asked us to stay here until they're finished looking around. Why don't you sit down?''

Bea walked around the counter toward the chair, then gasped in alarm when she started to fall. Ben caught her plump forearm and steadied her with an arm around her waist. She looked up at him in annoyance, then, when he kicked aside the clump of papers she'd stepped on to reveal part of the broken ribbon cartridge that had caused her to turn her ankle, she sighed and admitted grudgingly, "Thank you, young man. It seems you were right.''

He inclined his head. "You're welcome. Are you hurt?''

She leaned on him and flexed her ankle. "No, I'm fine, just clumsy.''

"Then I'd better help you to the chair.''

She frowned at his impertinence, then, looking into his eyes, apparently saw the amusement he was trying to conceal. "Your name again?'' she asked imperiously.

"Stratton," he replied. "Ben." He sat her in the chair, and she tossed her head back. He imagined what a handful she must have been at nineteen.

"Thank you, Ben," she said. "You may call me Bea.''

Certain an honor had been conferred on him that was restricted to very few, he accepted it with appropriate gravity. "Thank you, Bea. Ah, here's Karen with coffee.''

While Karen handed Bea a paper cup of coffee and offered her a pastry from a small tray she'd brought, Ben walked around to Georgia. Before she knew what he intended, he lifted her onto the counter. "You look as though you need to be off your feet," he said, seeing her surprised expression. "Try to relax. I know it's been a shock and the cleanup looks horrendous, but I'll stay around to help you."

Georgia wanted to scream and cry and carry on. She didn't want to sit and wait, all controlled and mature, while Phil and his partner went over her store. She wanted to knock down the few books that remained standing. She wanted to kick and rave about the cruel and selfish vandals who had done this to her. Something about Ben's strong hands lifting her onto the counter as though she weighed no more than a child, and the gentle empathy in his eyes, contributed to that feeling. Instead of making her feel stronger, he made her want to throw her arms around him and cry.

Ben took the coffee Karen offered him and handed it to Georgia. He smiled into her uncertain expression. "Think of it as a good excuse to ask the landlord to repaint."

She took the lid off her cup and gave him a dry glance. "Repainting inside isn't the landlord's job."

He shrugged, taking his own cup from Karen. "You've never had me for a landlord before."

Karen offered them the platter of pastry. "Our previous landlord wouldn't even paint the outside. Georgia, have an apple fritter. It looks like it's going to be a long day."

Georgia put her hand to her now queasy stomach. "I don't think I can eat anything." Then her frown deepened and she looked around. "But I had a blueberry muffin in a bag and a cup of coffee when I came to work this morning.''

Ben pointed behind him. ''I stepped over it. You must have dropped it when you saw what had happened.''

Karen put the platter on the work surface behind the counter. Then she came back around the counter and looked at Georgia. ''Do you think MacKay did this?''

''No,'' she said. Her expression and her voice registered surprise that Karen had suggested he was responsible. ''I know he thinks I'm an obstacle in the path of his financial success, but... I mean, we all went to school together—you and Wally and Rob and I. I can imagine him asking the city council to rezone this particular part of the block residential just so I'd have to move, but I can't imagine him doing—'' she waved a hand at the wanton destruction ''—this.''

Karen looked at Ben. ''She gives him too much credit. She does that with everyone. I don't like the looks of this.''

''Frankly, neither do I.'' Phil Hansen came to lean a hip against the counter while his partner went out to the patrol car. In his hands were the shreds of the green smock. ''Do you have any idea what this is about, Georgia?''

''No,'' she said, taking the smock from him. ''Isn't it just...vandals?'' The last word came out weakly as she held up the smock and saw the work a knife had done. She felt herself go pale.

Ben took the smock from her. ''Drink your coffee,'' he ordered quietly, then turned to Phil. ''Did you find anything?''

Phil held out a hand with several minute pieces of straw in it. ''A few pieces of this in the back room.

Otherwise, it looks like the usual under-the-street entry that's become part of our weekly routine around here.''

Ben frowned at him. ''What do you mean?''

''Astoria's built over the remnants of the turn-of-the-century city. There's an underground network of catacombs that provides entrance to most of downtown's basements for every punk, thief and vandal in the county. When life gets dull for the less reputable element in town, we can always count on a rash of break-ins. They've been working hot and heavy for the past few months.''

''Can't you seal off the underground?''

Phil shook his head. ''It would be an expensive proposition. The merchants think the city should do it and the city thinks it's the merchants' responsibility. Impasse. Anyway...'' He glanced at the mess behind him, bounced a look off Ben that Georgia couldn't quite decipher, then focused on her gravely. ''I don't like the look of this, Georgia. It isn't just random vandalism. It's aimed directly at you.''

''But, why?'' she asked. ''I know I've upset Rob MacKay, but I can't believe he'd do this.''

Phil smiled. ''Karen told me about the grant. Congratulations. Rob MacKay, huh? I'll talk to him.''

''He has horses,'' Karen said, standing beside her husband, her arms folded.

When everyone turned to her, waiting for her to explain that apparent non sequitur, she reached into her husband's hand to pick up a piece of straw between her thumb and forefinger and said, ''Straw is used in horse stalls.''

Phil smiled down at Karen. ''How'd you like to be a cop, lady? Great hours, great pay.''

She patted his cheek. "Then who'd make your doughnuts, flatfoot?"

Phil reclaimed the piece of hay and put it in his shirt pocket. "Good point. Georgia, maybe you should stay with someone for a while," he suggested, "until I can check this out a little further." He shook hands with Ben, winked at Georgia, kissed Karen's cheek and told her he'd see her at dinner.

As Phil went out to the patrol car, Karen gave Georgia a hug. "I'd better get back to work. You know, Phil was right about you staying with someone. Why don't you and the girls move into our family room?"

Georgia shook her head firmly. "Thanks, but I can't do that. We'd need something the size of the armory just for the girls' clothes for a few days."

"You're coming home with me," Bea said from her chair behind the counter. "And I won't hear any arguments."

Karen gave Georgia a silent, speaking look, then hugged her again. "Well, if you need anything at all, I expect you to call me."

Georgia followed her to the door and prepared to lock it, knowing she'd have to remain closed for the day to clean up. But a hand pushed against the door, and she found herself looking through the glass at Ragnar Jyhla. She opened the door for him and was instantly wrapped in his hug. He was a tall, spare man in jeans, a denim jacket and a baseball cap. A ruddy complexion, graying blond hair and a surprising impression of muscle for a man in his sixties spoke of Rags's Scandinavian ancestry and years spent at the helm of a ship. He and Bea had been seeing each other more than a year.

"Hi, Rags," Georgia said, reaching behind him to

lock the door. She drew him toward Ben. "I know Bea called you, but you didn't have to rush right over."

He looked around, his wrinkly lidded gray eyes widening at the mess. "Good God!" he gasped. "What happened?"

"The police think someone's out to get her." Bea walked into the arm he immediately curled around her. "She's going to stay with me for a while."

"Thank you, Bea, but I can't do that," Georgia said with as much determination as she could muster. She owed a lot to Bea, and more than that, she admired and respected her. Despite her mother-in-law's propensity for taking over, Georgia seldom fought her, knowing she meant well and was motivated by love for her and the girls. But this time she would have to be firm. She was about to offer several reasons why it was impossible, but was prevented from doing so by Rags, who appeared to be staring at Ben with a combination of surprise and pleasure.

"Rags, this is..." she began.

"Ben Stratton," Rags said, covering the small space that separated them and offering his hand. "The best backhand on the Portland Tennis Club courts. How the hell are you, and what are you doing here?"

Apparently as pleased to see Rags as the man was to see him, Ben laughed and shook hands with him as Georgia watched in surprise. "I'm great. Dave and I just bought this building," he said. "I happened to be around this morning when Georgia discovered the mess. I forgot that you live here part-time."

"River pilots usually have a foot at each end of their route. When I'm not in Portland, this is where you'll find me."

Ben glanced at his arm around Bea and grinned. "And you have a lady in every port along the way?"

Rags tightened his arm around her. "No, just this one. This is what happens to you when your friends can't stand your single status. They invite you to dinner, put a beautiful woman in your path and watch you try to weigh anchor."

Ben looked at his broad grin and appearance of general good humor. "You don't look as though you're suffering."

"He's never been better fed," Bea assured Ben, her chin angled, "or better cared for."

Ragnar frowned down at her. "Then why don't we make it permanent?"

Bea blushed and gave Rags a sturdy slap on the chest. "Rags, really. I explained that I have... responsibilities. I just can't run off to Portland. And this is not the place to discuss it."

Ragnar looked from Georgia to Ben. "We're among friends. I want you two to know we fought about this all over Mexico, and I want to go on record as having offered to make an honest woman of her." He shook his head at Ben and sighed with exaggerated regret. "Women are hard to deal with today. They have so many responsibilities that don't include us. How have we managed to slip in status?"

Ben laughed. "Apparently something got by us while we were playing tennis."

Bea cast a murderous glance from one man to the other. "We have a full day's work here, gentlemen. The sooner we begin, the sooner Georgia can get home and pack."

"We're not moving in with you, Bea," Georgia said, feeling almost too weary to face off against her mother-in-law. "The girls have all kinds of things going at school, and I can't disrupt them like that. I'm sure this was just somebody's crude attempt to...to frighten me. I'm sure they know it's worked, and now they'll leave me alone."

Bea squared her shoulders. "Georgia, Officer Hansen suggested that you need protection."

"My house is secure. We'll be fine."

"Think of the girls."

The safety of her daughters was enough to make Georgia think twice, but then she had to consider the danger she would face at the hands of her girls were she to suggest that they all move in with their grandmother. Bea would be after them to keep their music down, wear longer skirts, give up volleyball for more academic pursuits. It would never work.

"You're moving in with me," Bea said, "and that's final."

Seeing the look of desperation in Georgia's eyes, Ben suggested, "Why don't I move in with Georgia for a while?" When both women's eyes rose to his in alarm, he added easily, "I've decided to stay in town for awhile anyway. I have to see an architect and contractors, and working out of a motel room is less than convenient. You must have a spare room or an extra sofa." When Georgia said nothing but continued to stare at him as though he'd suggested they share a hot tub filled with champagne, he said, "A corner in the garage?"

"What I have," Georgia said, "are two teenage daughters to whom I am constantly preaching the value of exercising caution around men they don't know."

"I know him," Rags said quietly. "We play doubles in the tennis club's celebrity tournament every year to raise money for Waverley Children's Home." He grinned. "My wily trickery and his young legs are a deadly combination. We've even shared the court with the governor a time or two."

"But..." Bea began to protest.

"Face it, Beabee," Rags went on. "Ben could certainly provide better protection for Georgia and the girls than you could—unless, of course, we're dealing with a criminal who's susceptible to intimidation."

Georgia was surprised when Bea took no offense at Rags's suggestion or his teasing jab. She simply seemed to be considering the truth of what he's said. "I suppose his being seen with her might even discourage someone from threatening her further."

"Exactly."

"All right. Ben, you'll move in with Georgia and the girls tonight. Gary had a small workshop in a shed behind the house that hasn't been touched since he died. It has all the comforts of home. There." Dusting off her hands as though satisfied that was settled, Bea gave further orders. "Georgia, we'll need large plastic garbage bags to get some of this junk off the floor so we can assess the damage. You two youngsters can do the bending, while Rags and I record what you've lost for the insurance company and to facilitate your reordering."

As Ben and Ragnar righted a card rack and Bea sorted through the rubble for the cards that belonged on it, Georgia picked her way to the back room, where she kept garbage bags. Her thoughts and her feelings were too chaotic for her to analyze how she felt. The only thing that registered clearly was a sense of panic. Her daughter was troubled, her store had been trashed, it looked as though someone would take great pleasure in making her suffer unspeakable emotional and probably physical agonies, she was in charge of a countywide event that would bring thousands of people to Astoria, and a man she'd known for two days and had seen for probably a total of an hour in that time was moving in with her for an indefinite stay. The urge to cry and scream and kick had left her. Now she felt a desperate need to run away.

"HE'S GOING TO *LIVE* HERE?" Lacey blinked, looking at Linda to make sure she hadn't misunderstood.

Linda, who liked to get things straight, asked, "You mean, Mr. Stratton, your landlord, is moving in with us?"

Georgia abandoned the onion she was trying to chop and turned to the girls, who still wore their knee socks, athletic shorts and Astoria High volleyball shirts. "I mean that he's going to live in Daddy's shop until the police can find out who trashed the store."

"Why?" Lacey asked.

Trying to minimize the suggestion of danger to herself, Georgia turned back to the onion. "I don't know. Mr. Hansen suggested that someone stay with us. The other alternative was moving in with Grandma for a week."

Lacey thought a moment, then threw her arms around Georgia. "Thank you, Mom. I mean, I know how you are about men and everything, but we'd have died at Grandma's."

Ignoring the onion once again, Georgia frowned at her youngest. "How am I about men?"

"You don't like them," Lacey replied without hesitation. "I mean, I know you said you *liked* Mr. Stratton the other night, but you don't like him like we like boys. You think he's cute but you wouldn't want to marry him. Can you be considered an old maid even though you've been married once?''

"No," Georgia replied. "Just an old widow. Could you two get changed and set the table, please?''

When Lacey ran upstairs, Linda lingered a moment, putting her arm around Georgia's shoulders. "Are you in some kind of trouble, Mom?''

"Not exactly," she replied, slanting Linda a smile. "Mr. Hansen just thought it would be good for us to have a man around for a while.''

Linda nodded thoughtfully. "It would.''

Anxious to divert her from her concerns, hoping she'd want to discuss this morning's upset, Georgia asked, "Did you have a good day today?''

"Practice was a killer," Linda replied, reaching into the colander of vegetables draining in the sink and pulling out a slice of cucumber. "Shelly jammed her finger. That's because she always covers her face when the ball comes at her instead of trying to bump it back.''

"See that boy you told me about?''

"Yes." She took a carrot spear. "He just didn't see me. Story of my life. We're going to vote for Astoria High's Columbia River Days Princess tomorrow. Shelly thinks she'll get it.''

Georgia cupped the chopped onions in her hand, carried them to the frying pan on the stove and added them to a browning pound of hamburger. "That's modest of her," she said.

Linda followed her, shrugging. "She's just being realistic. She looks like Kim Alexis, she has a great body and wears a C cup. The guys'll all vote for her.''

Georgia stirred the onions into the hamburger and

sniffed the resulting aroma. "I thought you said a lot of the girls don't like her."

Linda stared thoughtfully into the pan, nibbling on the carrot spear. "The popular girls like her 'cause she's one of them. The girls in my crowd think she's a snot, but we don't have any power. And they don't understand her, anyway."

"What's to understand?" Georgia asked, remembering all the times Shelly had slighted Linda in one way or another. "She uses you when she needs help studying or preparing a project for cooking class."

"I know," Linda admitted without any apparent resentment. "But we kind of understand each other. Her dad's gone, too. I mean, he just left her mom, but Shelly hasn't seen him in two years, and that's kind of like he's dead. A lot of the other kids have stepfathers, but at least they have them. Shelly misses her dad, too. And her mom's never around."

Georgia stopped stirring to look down at Linda, now certain that her grief ran deeper and was more complicated than she'd ever expected. To her surprise, Linda grinned up at her, shaking her head as though Georgia were cause for amusement.

"You're so *intense*, Mom. It's not like I expect you to get married tomorrow because I miss Dad. I was just trying to explain to you how I felt. When you look all upset like that, it makes me not want to tell you."

"I want you to tell me how you feel," Georgia insisted, putting an arm around her shoulders. "Don't spare my sensitivities. Mothers get upset, they worry about their kids—it's our job. I just hate to think you're unhappy."

"I'm not unhappy," Linda said, stirring the mixture Georgia was ignoring. "I just get lonesome sometimes.

You are going to drain the fat off this before you add the spaghetti sauce?''

Knowing that was Linda's way of concluding the discussion, Georgia nodded, reaching overhead for a colander. ''Yes, Miss Fonda, I am. Go get changed for dinner.''

Linda started to run off, then stopped in the doorway to the back hall and the stairs. ''Did Lacey tell you about the cold water faucet?''

''No.''

''It wobbles. She tried to fix it, but it still feels a little weird to me.''

''All right. I'll have a look at it.'' Georgia drained the meat first, then, filling the coffee decanter, she had to give the faucet an extra turn in order to produce water. She frowned at it, considering the advantages of simply calling a plumber over trying to do something about it herself and saving the hundred dollars. A knock on the back door distracted her. ''Come in!'' she called.

Ben walked into the kitchen, looking freshly showered and very large. For an instant she remembered Gary walking in like that after a Saturday afternoon in his workshop, looking fresh and hungry. Startled by the memory, she couldn't speak for a moment.

''Your husband was a lucky man,'' he said, coming over to the sink, where she stood. ''That shop has every tool imaginable, a comfortable sofa, a television and a shower. My first apartment wasn't that elegant.''

''After college?'' she asked, making an effort to behave naturally. She opened the cupboard to her right, pulled out a jar of spaghetti sauce and twisted the lid.

''No, I was about sixteen and had gotten my first paycheck after working a month on a charter boat.''

When the lid refused to give, he took the jar from her, gave it a twist, then handed it back to her. It came off easily.

"You were on your own at sixteen?" she asked in some surprise. He had the look of a man who'd come from a privileged background.

"I was happy to be," he replied, his tone implying that was as far as he wished to discuss it. He leaned a hip against the counter while she went to the stove and added the sauce to the hamburger and onions. "Anything I can do to help?"

"The girls will be down in a minute to set the table. We will need another chair, though. There's a straight-backed one in the corner of the living room."

"Right." As he went off for the chair, Georgia took a moment to draw a deep breath, thinking that around him she always felt as though she had emphysema. She reached into a bottom cupboard for a large saucepan in which to cook the noodles, put it in the sink and turned the faucet on. Two things happened simultaneously. The faucet came off in her hand, and a spray of water the size of a whale's spout hit her in the face. Her scream was choked back by a mouthful of water as she groped blindly to cover the hole. Then a firm hand pushed her away and the rocket of water became a high-tension spurt under Ben's other hand.

Already as wet as she was, he turned his head to the girls, who now stood wide-eyed on the other side of the table. "Linda," he said calmly to Lacey, who was closest, "turn off the water supply in the basement."

"I'm Lacey," she replied, remaining where she stood.

Flinging her drenched hair back, Georgia heard his

frustrated half laugh. "Would you do it anyway, please?"

"I'll go." Linda ran down the basement steps, and the squeak of a seldom-used valve could be heard. The spurt of water under Ben's hand remained constant.

"Turn it the other way!" he shouted in the direction of the stairs.

After more squeaking, the flow of water stopped. He removed his hand carefully. A trickle of water escaped, then stopped completely. He turned to Georgia, the front of his shirt drenched, his face and hair dripping.

Looking as though she'd been completely submerged, Georgia smiled at him and asked, "Do you still think this'll be more convenient than your motel room?"

CHAPTER FIVE

BEN TRIED NOT to stare at the sight of Georgia eating spaghetti with a towel wrapped around her head. Without the distraction of her glossy hair, her eyes seemed wider, her cheekbones more pronounced, her smile more devastating. She continued to look at him warily, but the small crisis had eased the tension caused by his presence. And the five minutes it had taken him to replace a faucet washer and tighten the faucet handle had earned him a look of surprised respect from Georgia and her girls.

"Do you think you could fix our stereo?" Lacey asked clearing away dishes while Linda scooped ice cream into dessert glasses. "You have to turn it up really high to hear anything, and sometimes it makes this awful noise."

"Lacey..." Georgia began to scold.

"It's all right." Ben smiled across the table. "I'm a better plumber than an electrician, but I don't mind looking at it."

Linda distributed ice cream around the table, and both girls sat down again. "Why would you want to own a building in Astoria?"

"Because it's beautiful here," he replied. "Having business here will give me a good excuse to come up often."

"But it rains all the time," Lacey pointed out.

Ben shrugged. "I lived for a couple of years in Los Angeles, where it's sunny all the time. You can get tired of that, too."

Lacey looked doubtful. "Really? I'm going to have a farm in Bend, where it's sunny. And I'll have animals all over the place."

With the child's looks, Ben thought she might already be contemplating a modeling career in Paris. He thought it refreshing that she seemed unaware of her special beauty and longed for something as wholesome as a farm and animals.

"What about you?" he asked Linda.

"I'm going to have a restaurant and lots of kids," she replied. Then she slanted Georgia a teasing look. "And a dishwasher that works." Immediately after the words were spoken, she straightened in her chair, turned to Lacey, who seemed to read some message in her eyes, then both girls turned to Georgia and cried simultaneously, "He can fix the dishwasher!"

Georgia smiled apologetically at Ben. "I'm sorry. We've been handyman poor around here for a long time, and they're a little delirious over your skill." She darted a threatening look at Linda and Lacey. "Please don't touch the dishwasher, Ben. The girls aren't expected to do that much around here, and dishes for the three of us—well, four of us—isn't going to kill them."

"What's the matter with the dishwasher?" he asked.

Before Lacey could reply, Georgia cast her a quelling look. "It doesn't matter. It's as old as Lacey is. Probably just time to throw it away."

"And me, too, I suppose," Lacey teased.

Georgia smiled at her. "Not till after you've done the dishes."

When Ben insisted on looking at the girls' stereo after dinner, Georgia took a thermos of coffee and a space heater to the workshop to make it more comfortable. Spring in Astoria was cold and damp. The sofa didn't open into a bed, but she put sheets and an old comforter on it, then a doubled-over blanket on top of that. She left another folded at the end of it, then made a mental note to bring fresh towels.

When she returned to the kitchen, the strains of "Tony, Tony, Tony" came vibrating down the stairs clearly and with considerable volume.

"Just a loose wire," Ben reported.

Shaking her head at the end of the auditory peace the faulty stereo had provided, Georgia laughed softly. "Thank you so much for fixing it. I hope you'll think of me while you're safely removed from potential eardrum damage in the workshop."

He grinned at her and she fought an attack of breathlessness with sudden briskness. "I left a thermos in the workshop for you and a space heater. I'd appreciate it if you'd turn it off before you go to sleep. Wait here, and I'll get you some towels." Before he could say anything, she ran downstairs to the dryer and back up again. She handed him two dark blue bath towels and a washcloth, thinking that now, at least, she had a reason to be breathless. "Breakfast is at seven," she went on, "and there isn't usually a moment's leeway. We have getting ready for school and work timed down to the second."

He was being dismissed, Ben realized, and turned to the back door.

"Thanks for fixing the faucet and the stereo," Georgia said quickly. "Had I been alone with the girls, I'm sure we'd have drowned."

He smiled, opening the door. "I'm sure Bea would have held me personally responsible, and I shudder to think what I'd have suffered." He turned to leave, then hesitated a moment. "How long have Bea and Rags been seeing each other?"

Georgia smiled fondly. "Over a year. She loves to cook for him, and he loves to tease her, as you saw. She doesn't let anyone else get away with that."

"You think he'll talk her into getting married?"

Georgia shrugged. "Bea's pretty independent, and Rags is indulgent, but he doesn't let her push him too far. I suppose she wants to be sure. Meanwhile, I'm glad they have each other. Everyone needs someone to care about them."

Ben nodded agreement, able to attest to that truth firsthand. Reluctant to leave the cozy kitchen and Georgia's smile, he made himself smile and do just that. "See you in the morning," he said over his shoulder.

Moving to the back door window, Georgia watched him walk toward the shop, his long strides eating up the shaggy lawn, his tight, narrow hips in old jeans moving to the distracting rhythm of his easy pace. Suddenly aware of what she was doing, she slapped the small curtain down and ran upstairs to ask the girls to lower the music.

In the workshop, Ben did a slow circuit of the small room, hands in his pockets, getting a feel for the man who had once spent long hours working there. The pegboard wall of carefully placed tools showed that he'd taken care of his possessions, but there was a comfortably messy air about the rest of the place with which he could identify. A pile of chairs in the corner in various stages of dismemberment, an overturned, legless table and a strange-looking hoop on a broken stand, the use of which he couldn't imagine, stood around the shop, probably attesting to a very human tendency to procrastinate.

On the wall over his workbench, next to a two-year-old poster-sized calendar from Astoria Builders Supply, was a framed photo of Linda and Lacey taken on the front steps of the house. He leaned on the workbench for a closer look. On the steps behind them was a smiling Georgia, her head leaning on the shoulder of a man who sat beside her. Linda leaned back against his knees, squinting against the sun, and Lacey rested against Georgia, looking just as she did now, delighted with the world, though a little baffled by it. It was a beautiful family portrait capturing the love and confidence in each other he was sure must be the backbone of every solid home.

Ben felt an acute sense of jealousy mingled with awe and admiration. It was nice to know those things did exist, though they weren't part of his experience. He found it oddly comforting to know that Georgia and the girls had had a husband and father they had loved and on whom they'd been able to depend. It also made him more able to appreciate what they had lost and how bereft they must feel.

A nice guy had occupied this space, Ben thought as he moved restlessly across the room. A guy who'd loved his wife and kids and been loved in return. Jealousy nudged him again, but he smiled to himself as he walked back to the stack of chairs. He had long ago decided that bitterness was destructive and counterproductive, but a little jealousy never hurt. The world was full of things he couldn't have; he'd have to be dead not to resent it occasionally.

He picked up a chair that matched those around the

dining table and saw that it was missing a turned rung on the bottom. He found the piece in a pile of things beside the chair and carried both to the workbench. It was going to be a long evening, he decided. He might as well make himself useful.

BREAKFAST REMINDED BEN of a raid. In the old movies about the twenties, people were always running back and forth and screaming as the police burst through the door. When Ben rapped lightly on the kitchen door and got no answer, he turned the knob and found it unlocked. Lacey was running past, red hair flying, shouting, "You said I could borrow it!"

Linda followed her, a curling iron in her hands, half her dark hair bouncing with curls, the other half hanging straight. "You can't borrow my Generra! You've got your own new sweater. Oh, hi, Ben."

"Hi," he replied tentatively. "You guys all right?"

She smiled at him. "Lacey's going to be dead. Mom'll be down in a minute. Have some cereal."

As both girls disappeared upstairs, Ben went to the table, where a box of cereal and a carton of milk stood. Georgia ran into the kitchen in her stocking feet, wearing a silky blue blouse over a slip, adjusting an earring. At the sight of him, she stopped, gasped and closed her eyes.

"It's all right," he assured her quickly, putting a hand over his face. "I've closed my eyes." He had, but not before he'd had a deliciously tantalizing glimpse of thin, satiny fabric molded to slender hips and long thighs. "If you'll put a bowl and spoon on the table, I won't even look up until you've done what you came in to do. Incidentally, Linda is chasing Lacey with a curling iron. I just thought you should know."

He heard a small laugh. "She must have tried to borrow her Generra sweater."

He almost dropped his hand in surprise, then caught himself. "How did you know?"

He heard a bowl and spoon clatter onto the table. "I'm their mother." He heard the sound of liquid pouring, heard it a second time, then the sound of Georgia expelling a small sound of relief. "Ah, caffeine. Okay, Ben. Count to five, then you can open your eyes."

He dutifully counted to five and lowered his hand to find himself alone in the kitchen. There was a bowl, a spoon and a banana at his place, and a steaming cup of coffee. Music blared from upstairs, the telephone rang twice, and a black cat with large amber eyes leaped onto the table, rubbing against his elbow with bold familiarity as he poured milk into his cereal.

Linda reappeared, shooed the cat off the table, then dropped books and jacket at her place and poured herself a glass of juice. "Sorry about that," she said, smiling at Ben as she stood and drank her juice. "Midnight lives next door but likes to sleep in our basement. He comes up to see what we're eating."

Lacey appeared, dropped her things beside Linda's and scooped up the cat. "And meany always chases him away."

"Not away," Linda corrected. "Just off the table."

"Poor baby," Lacey cooed over him, holding him in one arm while she rummaged through a fruit bin near the stove and pulled out an apple. "Mom down yet?"

"Ah...just for a minute," Ben replied. "I don't think she was quite ready yet. Aren't you two going to eat anything?"

Linda looked at him in surprise and held up her glass. "Juice."

Lacey bit into the apple.

Georgia appeared a moment later, dotted each girl with a kiss, petted the cat and refilled her coffee cup. She glanced at her watch. "Good morning, Ben. You girls about ready?"

Both heads nodded and Midnight was deposited out the back door. Georgia ran from the room again, and when she reappeared wearing a gray jacket that matched her skirt, the girls were nowhere in sight.

Expecting her to be upset, he was surprised when she simply leaned against the back door and waited. "Brushing their teeth," she explained. Then she glanced at his sweater and slacks. "Are you coming with us?"

He took his leather jacket from the back of the chair. "I'm your bodyguard, remember?"

"Well, that doesn't mean you have to stay with me every minute." She opened the door as the girls thundered down the stairs, grabbed their things and ran out to the car. "Surely you must have things you want to do on your own."

He ushered her out and turned the lock before closing the door behind him. "What I have to do involves the building," he said, keeping pace with her hurried strides around the house to the driveway. "Fortunately, that's where you'll be."

Georgia halted in her tracks. "Your truck's in my way."

"I'll drive," he said, digging keys out of his pocket.

Georgia would have protested, but the girls ran delightedly to the truck, exclaiming over its size. "Wait till the kids see us arrive in a red four-by-four with custom wheels!'' Ben opened the passenger door and the girls scrambled in.

Finding Georgia still hesitating, Ben caught her hand and pulled her to the driver's side. "My skirt's too..." she began to explain, indicating the high step and the slim cut of her skirt.

Ben tossed her purse to Lacey, then lifted Georgia onto the seat. "Watch your head," he cautioned.

Completely ruffled, Georgia sat silently while Ben and the girls talked across her, Linda giving him directions to the high school. Georgia was so close to his body she felt painted onto him, and breathing became even more of a problem for her than usual when he was around.

Their arrival in the school's parking lot caused the stir among the kids the girls had predicted. Linda opened her door, and Georgia watched as a tall, dark-haired young man in a letterman's jacket came to help her down and concluded that he was the boy Linda had told her about. He seemed much more aware of Linda, Georgia thought, than the girl realized. There were four boys to help Lacey down, and Ben had to wait a moment while an appreciative group walked around the truck and asked a few questions.

It wasn't until they'd headed back to town and Ben stopped at a red light, then glanced down at her that Georgia realized she was still painted to his side.

"You made their day," she said casually, scooting over.

He studied her for a moment, his eyes moving distractedly over her mouth, then her hair. "You should seriously consider a twenty-four-hour guard for them," he said, turning back to the road and accelerating when the light changed. "They're a dangerous combination of beauty and warmth. Did you have anything this morning besides that coffee?''

''No. I never do. Except an occasional blueberry muffin.''

He sent her a frowning glance, then looked back at the road. ''You look a little peaked this morning. Didn't you sleep well?''

''No,'' she replied again. ''But I never do that, either. It's nothing unusual. I have one of those systems that runs on coffee and adrenaline.''

''You open at nine-thirty?'' he asked, glancing at his watch.

Second-guessing him, Georgia turned in her seat to face him. ''Yes, but I usually use the extra hour to catch up on paperwork or check in stock. I have stuff downstairs I've been trying to check in and bring upstairs since the day you turned up in the basement. I've got to get to it.''

''Why can't you do it later today?''

''Because I work alone,'' she explained patiently. ''I can't work downstairs when a customer could walk in and need my help or rip me off. And the boxes are too heavy for me to carry upstairs and work on them in the shop.''

''I'll carry them up for you and help you check them in,'' he volunteered, turning into the parking lot of the Dutch Cup, a neat little restaurant with a view of the river. ''You know, it's not good for your girls to choke down juice and rush off to school.''

Georgia sighed. ''Did Bea coach you to say this? I'd rather they had solid breakfasts, but they're at a point in their lives when they'd rather make sure their hair is perfect than eat breakfast from the required food groups. I always make sure they have enough money to eat well from the cafeteria at lunch.''

He pulled into a parking spot and turned to grin at her. ''What do you do for lunch with no one to relieve you or run out to get you something.''

''I always have a granola bar in my purse,'' she replied.

Ben rolled his eyes, pushed his door open and jumped down. He turned to reach for her to help her down. She drew back, her expression suddenly haughty. As that was something he hadn't seen in her, he leaned an arm on the truck frame and waited.

''You're my landlord,'' she said evenly, ''not my husband. I haven't had to answer to anyone or do anything I haven't wanted to do in a long time. I'm comfortable with that. If we're going to be spending time together for the next few days, you're going to have to come to terms with it.''

Because she had spoken so calmly and so rationally and Ben had proved himself so far to be a rational man, Georgia fully expected him to get back in the truck and drive her to the store. Instead, he took hold of her arm, pulled her toward him and lifted her down.

''I'm also your bodyguard,'' he said quietly into her startled expression. ''And I'm a conscientious man. I feel as responsible to protect your inner body as I do your lovely arms and legs. If I carry you in there slung over my shoulder, we'll probably upset everyone.'' He locked the truck door, slammed it, then put an arm around her shoulders and started for the restaurant. ''So let's be civilized, all right?''

Ben had finished his breakfast and Georgia was halfway through a cheese omelet and toast before she could bring herself to speak to him. She was definitely annoyed by his presumption, but her feeling of confusion was stronger. It had been a long time since anyone— a man, particularly—had forced her into anything because he cared. Gary had been kind and gentle, though fairly forceful, and she'd forgotten the luxury of being that precious to someone. It was unsettling and curiously exciting to be outwitted by a man who had your best interests at heart.

"It could be," Ben said, "that you don't sleep well because you don't eat right."

"I don't sleep well," Georgia said, "because I've no one to sleep with." She heard the words come out of her mouth and looked up at him, daring him to misunderstand what she meant. When she saw that he didn't, her confusion deepened.

"I can only imagine the depth of your loss," he said gently. "I'm sorry."

She felt tears scrape her throat and sting her eyes. She sniffed them back, took a last sip of coffee and prayed they wouldn't fall. "Are you ready?"

"Why do you do that?" he asked, making no move to leave.

"What?" she asked wearily.

"Get angry when someone understands how you're feeling." When she hesitated over an answer, he took a guess. "Because you don't understand yourself, maybe? Because you run around so frantically so you don't have time to analyze it?"

Georgia tried not to react in any way that would betray how on target he was. She replied coolly, "Because my deepest feelings are hard for me to share. Particularly with a man I've known all of three days. Why do *you* do that?"

"What?"

"Come to my defense like a storybook hero? This is real life, you know. I'm a widow who pines for her husband. There's no future in this for you, if that's your plan."

He studied her a moment, then gave her a smile that made her feel young and silly. "It's interesting that a woman wants to be accepted on her own terms, and when a man does that, she's sure he has sexual motives. You were in a mess and I wanted to help you. Now that I own your building, our financial futures are somewhat entwined. In helping you, I'm helping myself."

Georgia looked into his steady hazel gaze and found no reason there to disbelieve him. What was the matter with her? she wondered a little worriedly. Had all her social skills atrophied? "I'm sorry," she said with a sigh. "That didn't sound very grateful, did it?"

He grinned and stood, offering her a hand up. "No need to be grateful. Just don't accuse me of lechery. I'm very sensitive."

Ben paid for their breakfast, then walked Georgia out into the parking lot. He stopped at a newspaper box, digging in his pocket for change. "Let's see if there's anything in the paper about—" The sight of Georgia, halted and turned toward him in the middle of the driveway, and a speeding Camaro, bouncing over the sidewalk toward her, stopped him in midsentence.

Ben heard the roar of the car's powerful engine and saw Georgia's look of confusion then fear as she saw the car barreling down on her. He took two long strides, then threw himself at her as the car burst past them, twisting his body to take the brunt of the impact as they crashed to the ground.

Ben lay still for a moment, waiting for his heart to settle down, his primary relief the comforting weight of Georgia's body atop his. He could feel her heart pounding against his and see the lingering shock in her eyes when she braced herself with a forearm on his chest and looked down at him.

"It occurs to me," she said gravely, as people began to run toward them from the restaurant, "that as a bodyguard, you're underpaid."

CHAPTER SIX

"GEORGIA, I DON'T KNOW what the hell is going on."
Phil made notes on his small pad while leaning against
the open door of Ben's truck. Georgia sat sideways on
the passenger seat, her legs hanging down so that her
feet, one of them shoeless, rested on the chrome running board. "You didn't even get a glimpse of the
driver?"

"It happened too fast," Ben said, leaning against the
truck's frame. "It was a Camaro, but it never occurred
to me to look up at the driver."

"If Ben didn't have good reflexes," Georgia told
Phil quietly, "I'd be dead, or very messy."

"MacKay's out of town," Phil said. "Has been
since the day of the Downtown Enrichment Association
meeting. We have no idea where he went. He seems
to have disappeared."

Ben straightened. "Convenient. He could have hired
someone to trash her shop and run her down."

Phil raised an eyebrow and flipped the pad closed.
"That's possible. He's a hothead with big ideas, and I
know he and Georgia have gone head-to-head over a
few things, but somehow this just doesn't seem like his
style. Meanwhile—" he slapped Ben on the chest with
the pad "—good work. Keep it up till I find out what's
going on here." He leaned into the truck, kissed Georgia's cheek, then joined the officer who was taking a

statement from the woman who'd seen the incident from the restaurant window.

Georgia looked up at Ben hopefully. "Did you find my shoe?"

He shook his head, a little concerned by her utter calm. "Apparently it flew off your foot when I grabbed you. The lady sitting by the window said she saw the car hit it midair. It could be in the river."

That information suggested the hairbreadth by which Georgia had missed being hit and the impact with which the car would have struck her. Since their stop at the restaurant was not part of her usual routine, the attack suggested she had been followed from home. She looked up at him, that reality reflected in her eyes. But her only reaction was a sigh. She swung her legs into the truck. "Well, I'm already half an hour late opening. Breakfast was a great idea, Ben."

Georgia stared straight ahead while Ben continued to study her a moment before closing her door and walking around the truck. As he drove silently to the shop, Georgia knew he was the only reason she was alive at this moment. Still, the suggestion to stop for breakfast had been his, and it was easy and comfortable to blame him. She didn't understand and couldn't quite believe what was happening to her. Shifting responsibility for it onto someone else relieved her of the burden.

Wearing the low-heeled shoes she always kept at the store, Georgia worked like a demon. Ben carried box after box up from the basement for her, then checked items off the invoice as she unwrapped her purchases and read their stock numbers. Otherwise, they didn't speak at all.

Ben left shortly after one, and Georgia tried to ignore

his absence, imagining him back at the workshop, packing his bags. That was fine, she told herself. She'd gotten along before he'd come to town.... Of course, no one had been trying to kill her then. The telephone rang before that fact could settle in her mind and destroy the fragile composure she'd constructed over frayed nerves. It was John Kirby, the owner of Estuary Architects. He wanted to make an appointment with her and Karen to discuss the design of the building's new face.

She frowned, wondering why he wanted to speak to her. Apparently sensing her confusion, the gentleman on the other end said, "Mr. Stratton called me. He said he'd like the two of you in on the discussion. This afternoon okay? About two-thirty?"

"Yes, I think so," Georgia replied. "I'll call Mrs. Hansen to be sure. But I'm not sure about Mr...."

At that very moment the bell over her door tinkled, announcing the arrival of a customer. She looked up to see Ben closing the door behind him, a large white bag balanced on one hand. Guilt and remorse filled her. She held the receiver against her chest. "It's Estuary Architects. They want to know if it's all right to come by at two-thirty this afternoon to talk to us."

He placed the bag on the counter beside her, and she got a subtle whiff of a beefy scent. He wore the same neutral expression he'd worn since they'd driven back to the shop. It made her feel deprived and uncertain. "Is it all right with Karen?" he asked.

"I'll check with her." Into the receiver, she said, "It's fine with Mr. Stratton. I'll check with Mrs. Hansen. If you don't hear from me, two-thirty will be fine."

A call to Karen brought the same reaction Georgia had experienced. "He wants to talk to *us*?"

"Yes," Georgia replied, unwilling to admit her own surprise with Ben standing two feet away, pulling paper cups out of the bag.

"Why?"

"Oh, our valuable input, I'm sure," she replied casually. "Can you be here?"

"You bet. I'll bring coffee and cookies."

"Great." Georgia replaced the receiver and smiled brightly at Ben. "She'll be here."

"Good." He handed her a tub-shaped cup, his index fingers holding several packages of crackers to the lid. "Beef barley soup."

"Thank you." She took it from him, removed the lid and sniffed the wonderful aroma of beef and vegetables. A shopper came to the counter with a thin volume of poetry. Georgia rang up the sale, bagged the purchase and sent the customer on her way with a smile. Then she turned to Ben. He leaned a hip on the counter and sipped from the cup. "I thought you'd left to go back to the workshop and pack your things."

He raised an eyebrow. "Why?"

"Because I was so rude and ungrateful."

His hazel gaze held hers for a moment, his expression remaining quiet. He shrugged. "We storybook heroes deal with dragons all the time."

"I'm sorry."

"Forget it."

Not entirely satisfied that the comfortable communication she'd come to enjoy with him had been reestablished, Georgia pushed a little harder. "You're still angry."

"I'm not angry," he denied. Then he looked at her,

the first frank look he'd given her in hours. "Hurt, maybe."

She nodded, accepting that he had a right to be. "I don't blame you. In my own defense I can only say I was frightened and upset, and I'm not used to someone caring. Oh, I have great friends, but I mean..." She drew a breath and admitted honestly, "I'm not used to a man caring."

"Then we're both confused." He reached into the bag and brought out two wide-bowled plastic spoons, handing her one. "I'm not used to caring. I can't explain my motives because I don't understand them. But I can promise you they hold no danger for you."

Georgia sighed, satisfied they were on an even footing again. Honesty seemed to be what they shared best.

It didn't occur to either of them that he could be wrong.

JOHN KIRBY'S PLANS for the Roberts Buildings' facelift brought smiles to Georgia's and Karen's faces as they studied the blueprint spread out on Georgia's counter. Kirby indicated the roofline with his pen. "The face will be weathered-look board and batten. If you don't mind giving up your big display windows, I'd suggest that we put in bay windows of small-paned glass—the bookstore's on the west side and the bakery's on the east. I suggest you removed your old awnings and build out a boardwalklike roof or put a shingled roof over the bays. Replace your commercial doors with ones typical of the atmosphere." He turned to Ben. "I'd use stone up to the windows, but that would be expensive."

Georgia and Karen looked at each other again in

wonder, then turned simultaneously to Ben. "Well?" he asked.

Georgia was speechless. Karen never suffered from that condition. "The plan is more than either of us ever hoped for. We were ready to settle for fresh paint." She put a hand on the blueprint. "This would be exquisite, but don't bankrupt yourself."

Ben nodded. "I have to talk it over with my uncle, but I wanted to make certain you two approved before I took it to him." He turned to Kirby. "I'll let you know tomorrow afternoon."

Karen left in a daze, and Georgia finished the day that way. As she rearranged the window with new stock, Georgia tried to imagine a neat bay window of small-paned glass, herself looking out on a barrel of flowers near her door. It was what she and Karen dreamed of—class and elegance. And they weren't going to have to mortgage their homes to get it.

It was almost four when Linda burst through the shop door, her books clutched to her chest, her purse and gym bag hanging crazily from her arm. "Guess what?" she demanded.

Georgia looked from Linda to Lacey, who'd gone behind the counter to put her books and bags down, to Linda's friend Shelly. Georgia's gaze lingered a moment on Shelly's platinum elegance. The girl always made her feel that her daughter was keeping company with Lolita. Georgia looked at Linda again, wondering what could possibly have put that flare of excitement in her eyes. Then she remembered the pageant.

"You were chosen as Astoria High's Columbia River Days Princess!" Georgia guessed.

Linda rolled her eyes, and Shelly looked at Georgia as though she were crazy. "*I* got that, Mrs. Madison."

Of course.

"Ms. Moss put me in charge of the high school's cookie concession for Columbia River Days!"

"Oh!" Georgia tried to look delighted, though that sounded like a lot of work to her. But Linda loved work. "Darling, that's wonderful."

"I've got to plan what we're going to make and figure out a budget. Can I use the adding machine in your office?"

"Of course."

The two girls headed for the stairs, then Linda stopped in her tracks and Shelly collided with her. "Mom, we have to go grocery shopping before we go home," Linda said urgently. "I want to try some recipes tonight."

Georgia turned to Ben, who was just coming up the basement stairs with the last box of freight. "Ben drove this morning, honey. You'll have to ask him."

Ben looked in puzzlement from Georgia to Linda, his glance hesitating for a moment as it passed over Shelly. "Ask me what?"

Georgia watched in delight as Linda went through her "Guess what?" routine all over again. The girl had been so serious about things since her father's death. It somehow restored Georgia's faith in herself as a mother to see Linda reacting with youthful excitement and anticipation—the fact that it was all generated by a responsibility she was anxious to execute well was a mother-bonus.

"All *right*!" Ben grinned at Linda. "Good for you."

"I need to get some stuff at the store before we go home so I can try some recipes tonight. Mom says since you drove..."

He nodded before she could finish. "Sure. No problem."

"Thanks." Beaming, Linda headed for the office, Shelly following.

As Ben carried the box to the floor behind the counter where Georgia had cleared a spot, Lacey hiked herself onto the safe and folded her arms, her long legs dangling. "Are you sure she's ours?" she asked.

Georgia knelt beside the box as Ben slit it open with a knife blade. She smiled up at Lacey. "I've often suspected you were both left by alien storks. Why?"

Lacey pointed a hand in disgust in the direction in which her sister had disappeared. "She came in second to Hot Hips for pageant princess, and she's not even upset about it. But they put her in charge of all that *work* and she's happy!"

Georgia was so surprised by the news that Lacey's forbidden name for Shelly went unnoticed. "She was runner-up?"

"Yeah." Lacey shook her head. "She doesn't get anything for that, but it means she was *almost* a princess. Instead, she's got all that work to do. Her whole cooking class is excited about it now, but when it comes time to do it all, nobody'll want to help her and she'll have to do it herself." Lacey frowned at Georgia. "Linda's weird sometimes, you know? I'm going to Columbia Chocolates for some macadamia clusters. Anybody want anything?"

As Lacey loped off, Georgia stared worriedly in the direction of her office.

"What's the matter?" Ben asked, pulling the packing slip off and pressing the sides of the box flaps open.

"She was almost a princess," Georgia said wistfully, not even realizing until that moment that she harbored every mother's secret wish that her daughter be recognized for the grace and beauty she knew she possessed.

"You're wrong about that," Ben said.

She turned to him in surprise.

"That's the sweetest, most responsible kid I've ever seen," he explained. "She is royalty. And that football jock who helped her out of the truck this morning knows it, too."

IF THERE WAS SUCH A THING as orderly chaos, Georgia decided at nine o'clock that night, her kitchen was it. Every flat surface had a bowl or a cookie tin on it, and anyone foolish enough to wander in when delicious aromas began to radiate from the room had been pressed into service. The flour sprinkled on the counter to facilitate the rolling out of butter-cookie dough had filtered onto the floor and drifted into the air. Sprinkles and chocolate chips crunched underfoot, and there was so much coconut everywhere that it looked as though a condor nest had exploded overhead. But Linda was humming, Lacey was cooperating happily, and Ben stood nearby applying muscle to stiff chocolate-chip cookie batter. Georgia had a strong sense of all being right in her world.

Pressing out heart-shaped cookies, she waited until Linda turned her back to put a tray in the oven, then reached her index finger into the chocolate-chip batter and put it into her mouth.

Ben slanted her a scolding glance. "I don't think that's allowed," he cautioned quietly.

"Of course it is," she whispered. "I'm the mother."

"Isn't that abuse of authority?"

She frowned at him. "We're talking about chocolate-chip cookie dough, Ben. Marquess of Queensbury rules don't apply.'' She looked into his curious expression and guessed, ''You've never had cookie dough, have you?''

''Never had a mother who made cookies.''

Without pausing to think, Georgia ran the index finger of her left hand along the top of the dough and put it up to his mouth. The suggestive quality of what she was doing did occur to her then, but it was too late. His eyes settled on hers for one lengthy, lazy moment, then he dipped his head. She felt the slightest graze of his teeth, the barest touch of his tongue as he nipped the dough off her finger, then the soft warmth of his lips as he closed his mouth and drew away.

Struggling desperately to maintain her equanimity when her entire body reacted to that small touch of his mouth, she asked calmly, ''Well?''

He closed his eyes to consider. ''Good stuff,'' he agreed, then he opened his eyes and looked at her again, a dangerous light in their depths. ''But served that way, you could make me beg for cat food.''

It was well after eleven when the kitchen had been cleaned up and they all sat around the table sampling cookies.

''The chocolate sandwiches are the best,'' Lacey voted enthusiastically.

Georgia examined the perfectly round shape of the powdered-sugar-covered confection in her hand. ''I like the Russian tea cakes.''

''What are these called?'' Ben asked of a macaroon-like cookie he held between thumb and forefinger.

''Kisses,'' Linda replied.

Georgia could not explain the sudden tension that surrounded her. She waited, her breath caught in her throat so that she dared not bite into the tea cake. Waves of awareness emanated from Ben, though he did little more than push the plate of cookies toward her. "Try one," he suggested. "You're in for a treat."

Georgia glanced at him, saw that dangerous look still alive in his eyes and returned her attention to the tea cake she held. The girls, in discussion over whether the chocolate sandwiches needed more or less filling, noticed nothing.

"I'm stuffed, thanks," she said evenly.

He pulled the plate back toward him. "Too bad," he said. "You're missing out."

"Mom, do you think I should go for real butter in the butter cookies?" Linda nibbled at a heart-shaped cookie, then broke the point off and handed it across the table. "The added expense would mean I'd have to cut back one kind of cookie."

Lacey bit into a dark, square cookie and grimaced. "You can scratch the prune bars."

"But save the kisses," Ben said.

Georgia looked up at him, warning him with her eyes. The girls had noticed nothing yet, but they were frighteningly astute. "These are delicious, but they'll be heavenly with real butter."

"I was thinking we'd frost half and leave half plain for people wanting less sugar."

Georgia nodded approval. "I'd say you're off to a great start, Lindy."

"Wouldn't you make more money," Lacey asked, "if you just made a whole bunch of the fancy, frosted ones?"

"Maybe," Linda replied, "but it's a project for all the cooking classes, and believe it or not, there are a few guys in them. And some girls who cook like Mom.''

Georgia turned at that remark, her frown threatening. Linda laughed. ''With skill, but not a lot of enthusiasm. Anyway, bar cookies are easier for them to do, and they're usually full of stuff the guys like to eat. Drop cookies and refrigerator cookies are good for the kids who are better bakers, and those of us who love to bake will do the fancier stuff.''

''Well-thought-out plan, Linda,'' Ben said with a sincerity that brought a blush to her face. ''You'll probably be ready to compete with Mrs. Fields by the time you're out of high school.''

Lacey leaned across the corner of the table toward her sister. ''Aren't you even a little upset that you didn't get princess? I mean, you came so close. And Shelly got it.''

''It's kind of neat that I got so close,'' Linda admitted, ''but if I'd gotten it, I'd have died. For a whole week before the pageant, the princesses from each of the high schools go around to all the service clubs and give talks about Columbia River Days.'' When Lacey failed to see the cause for her relief, Linda said plainly, ''Public speaking, Lace! I hate that! You get to act like a princess the night of the pageant and the dance that opens the weekend, but all those other times I'd be scared to death. That's not for me. I'd rather bake behind the scenes.''

Lacey looked at Georgia. ''See what I mean? Weird.''

Georgia smiled fondly at both of them. ''You'd better get to bed. It's almost midnight.''

Lacey stretched. ''Tomorrow's Saturday.''

"You still have volleyball practice. And no music tonight, please. It's too late."

Lacey smiled at Ben as she stood and pushed her chair in. "The tape player sure works great, Ben. Now it's got *lots* of volume."

Linda laughed, following her sister toward the stairs. "Bad for Mom's nerves, but we love it."

Georgia waved the girls off and found herself in the suddenly silent kitchen, an arm's reach away from the man who had been making playful, suggestive remarks all evening. She tried to look severe, but her pulse was skipping. "That's dangerous," she said.

"What?" His look of innocence made her wonder if she had imagined his teasing.

"I keep my personal life very circumspect," she replied a little stiffly, angry now that she might have misunderstood. Or was she disappointed? "My girls see and hear everything and understand more than that. Teasing me about kisses is...is..."

"Dangerous," he supplied for her, and she knew suddenly that she hadn't imagined a thing. He leaned toward her on an elbow, his eyes warm and frank. "Because they might think their mother is interested in a man? Or because you might discover that you are?"

"My man is dead," she said calmly.

Ben studied her, trying to decide if that was simply a defense mechanism or if she was as sincere as she sounded. "Then, isn't it time you found another?"

For an instant, he thought he saw longing in her eyes. Then she closed them and shook her head. "No."

"Why?" He knew he was pushing. As a rule he didn't like his own space invaded and made it a point to keep at least an elbow's distance from everyone else's. But some kind of strange magnetism surrounded this woman and drew him.

"Because..." Georgia wanted to explain but couldn't find a way to state simply what had become such a complex burden. "He died unexpectedly. There was so much between us that's just—" she spread both hands in a gesture of helplessness "—unfinished, I guess."

He reached out to enclose her wrist in his fingers. "Georgia, Gary is dead. What you had is over. You can't leave the rest of your life unfinished because of that."

Her hand lay quietly under his. He had expected her to yank it away impatiently or wriggle free of his grip to make her point. She simply looked at him with a sadness so grave that he opened his hand. "I have the girls and some lovely memories," she said.

"In a couple of years," he said gently, "they'll be off to college, and if the male population of this country is in its right mind, they'll have families of their own before you know what happened. Then all you'll have will be the memories. What then?"

She pushed her chair back and gathered up cups. She gave him a look of resignation with a little laughter behind it. "Then I guess it's my shawl and my rocking chair in the sun on the porch of some convalescent home."

Exasperated but not discouraged, he helped her clean up. "I'll bet you've even forgotten what it's like," he said, putting the carton of milk back in the refrigerator.

"What?"

"Being kissed."

She turned from the sink in surprise, wet hands held away from her body as he walked toward her, a dish towel in his hands. His even, hazel gaze held hers as he stopped inches away.

"Of course I haven't. Gary was always so..." She paused, expecting the memory of being in Gary's arms to waft around her as it always did, sharp and clear and painful. But it wouldn't form. She frowned, trying to help it along. "Kisses never became perfunctory between us. They were always warm and..."

It occurred to him that this wasn't the way he wanted to kiss her. He'd read that search for the memory in her eyes and guessed by the surprise and disappointment there that she hadn't found it. It proved his point but put him in the position of being a reassurance to her rather than allowing him to play any of the other dashing, more romantic roles he had in mind. Still, he experienced a vague surprise when his mind pushed aside any disappointment he might have felt and decided that being what she needed was a place to start.

He handed her the towel and waited while she dried her hands. Then he put a hand under the short, silky hair at the back of her neck and pulled her closer, bridging the few inches that separated them. She didn't resist. Her hands flattened against his chest, not to hold him away, but as though she weren't quite sure what to do with them. Her soft, dark eyes were still confused, still unfocused, in search of a memory. He put his other arm around her and leaned down to close his mouth gently over hers.

There. That was it. Georgia gave herself over to the memory of warm, gentle lips, a hand in her hair, arms that were strong and protective. Warmth and tenderness filled her...and relief that she hadn't forgotten. Settling into the familiar comfort, feeling his flash of response, she pushed her hands up his chest and over his shoul-

ders to twine in his baby-fine hair. That was what finally alerted her. The hair in her fingers was wiry and
curly, and her arms were stretched farther than had
been required to hold Gary.

She came to full awareness with a little start, drawing her arms down and looking into Ben's now very
gold eyes in surprise. But he didn't free her and she
didn't struggle.

"Now that you know I'm not Gary," he said quietly,
"do you want to try that again?"

Georgia couldn't have said what made her raise her
arms to him a second time. There was something familiar in the tender way he held her, in every sure but
gentle move that lent a certain comfort to the promise
of excitement, a safety to the tantalizing threat of danger. Ben wasn't Gary, but he had goodness in common
with him and an appeal for her that was uniquely his.

The prideful edge of distance Ben had planned to
maintain in the kiss, to let her know he wouldn't be
mistaken for her husband a second time, melted when
she raised her arms to him. It dissolved completely
when she leaned her body against his in total trust,
parted her lips and waited for his.

Ben had never gone into a kiss with his spine like
oatmeal. He liked to have charge of a relationship, even
just an encounter, but power was the last thing on his
mind at the moment. He felt a responsibility here he
didn't entirely understand, and it made him go carefully. He sensed that Georgia needed kindness more
than passion, a reminder of what she was missing rather
than full-blown evidence.

As his mouth closed gently over hers, Georgia tasted
a hint of coffee, a suggestion of coconut and the very
distinctive flavor of man. After two years without even

a kiss, the headiness of it struck her like a blow. The tingling sensation brought on by fingers moving against her scalp, the delicious feeling of hands roving her back, brought back a host of things ignored and forgotten in the past two years. Even clinging to Ben as her senses were assaulted, she realized she was recalling not memories of Gary but memories of her own femininity, those emotional parts of her person that had been tucked away with her husband's clothes.

Though her mind was cautioning her to be careful, her body seemed to revel in its renewal, as though celebrating the restoration of its missing components. That was what this kiss felt like, she thought in wonder, a celebration.

Without understanding what was happening to her, or to himself, for that matter, Ben felt the newness. He had certainly never experienced this before—this promise of something wonderful curiously coupled with the patience to pursue it slowly. He raised his head while his body wanted more, amazed at his own restraint. He looked down into her brown eyes and smiled, pleased they were now focused—on him. "So I was wrong. You do remember."

She smiled up at him. "Ben," she said. That was all.

As he walked back to the workshop in the cool, breezy night, he knew what she meant. It had been a simple reassurance that she knew he wasn't Gary.

CHAPTER SEVEN

"HAVE YOU HAD HIM fill out a W-4 yet?" Karen asked Georgia. "Ben certainly seems to be working for you."

It was a quiet weekday afternoon, the first sunny day after a week of rain. Georgia and Karen had concluded earlier that all their customers were working in their gardens instead of shopping. The two women leaned on Georgia's counter, sipping coffee and watching the scaffolding being erected in front of the building. Through the window, they could see Ben in discussion with John Kirby and Wally Bishop.

"He's here with you every day, does all your heavy work, runs out for your lunch and coffee." Karen turned to grin at her. "Is there something developing here that I should know about?"

Georgia sighed. "This is all your husband's fault for saying in front of Bea that the girls and I shouldn't be alone. When the alternatives were moving in with her or letting Ben move in with us, the latter seemed more desirable. Now I'm not sure."

Karen toyed with a pencil on the counter, rolling it forward and back. "Is the widow's wall beginning to fall?"

Georgia glanced at her friend with a moue of disapproval. "It isn't a wall, Karen. How can I embark on a relationship when I don't know what went wrong with the other one? Or even if anything did?"

Karen ignored her dilemma and focused on the information that intrigued her. "So there is potential for a relationship here?"

Without warning or time to try to hold it back, a rosy glow climbed from Georgia's neck. Karen saw it and smiled. "What happened?" she demanded.

"Nothing momentous," Georgia lied. It shouldn't have been momentous, but it was.

"What?" Karen asked. "What?"

"He kissed me," Georgia reported simply, clearing her throat and shrugging. "That's all."

"That's all?" Karen put an arm around her shoulders and squeezed. "That's everything! You're coming back to us! Georgia..."

Taking exception, Georgia frowned at her friend. "I wasn't dead, Karen."

"No, but you had definitely retired." Karen squeezed her again. "What do the girls think of him?"

"It doesn't matter," Georgia insisted, trying to defuse Karen's excitement. "Sometime soon Ben will have to go back to Portland."

Karen recognized her evasion. "They like him, don't they?"

Georgia took the pencil from her and tossed it into her pencil cup. "He fixes breakfast every morning and they take time to eat it. He repaired the kitchen faucet, their stereo and the dishwasher. He knows a lot about volleyball." She frowned at Karen in concern. "I think they must have ordered him from God."

"Maybe God sent him," Karen suggested quietly, "because He wanted to do something nice for you. Maybe it's time to forget about how Gary died and move on."

Georgia straightened and looked levelly at Karen.

"If it had been Phil in those circumstances, could you just put it aside and get on with your life?"

Karen returned her even gaze. "If there was little chance of ever finding out the truth, I would. You have to think of yourself. Anyway, the more you hold on to that, the greater chance you have of the girls finding out." When Georgia looked at her in alarm, she said implacably, "I'm sorry, but you've got to face it. You've been lucky so far. Those few of us who know would never breathe a word, but you know how those things happen. A careless word is overheard, a kid tells another kid, someone at school thinks Linda and Lacey know and it comes out. Let it go, Georgia. Let yourself get serious about Ben Stratton."

The girls finding out the strange circumstances surrounding Gary's death was her worst nightmare. They'd worshiped him. Through their teens and as long as she could maintain it, she wanted their memory of him as the perfect, loving father to remain intact. She had held stubbornly to her own memory of him as the perfect, loving husband, though she admitted to herself in dark, private moments that she had a particle of doubt.

"Come on," Karen said bracingly. "I didn't mean to upset you. I just want you to start thinking about yourself for a change. You don't think your firm bosom and tight bottom are going to last forever, do you? Pretty soon you'll get saggy and wrinkled, and even the garbage man won't look at you twice."

Georgia glared at Karen. "Don't you have to get back to work?"

"No," Karen replied blandly. "I'm yours for as long as you need me. You're so lucky."

"Is that what you call it?"

Suddenly another figure appeared in the window, stopping to talk to the men outside. It was Phil.

"Hi," he said as he came through the door. To Karen, he added, "Thought I'd find you here."

"Don't tell me," Karen sighed. "You're not coming home tonight. A stakeout or a raid or a big bust or something."

Phil frowned in mock confusion. "I don't think there's a woman with a big bust in this town."

"Ha, ha." Karen made a face at him. "So which is it?"

"You were right the first time," he replied, hooking an arm around her. "A stakeout. I won't be home until late."

"Don't get hurt," she ordered, "or I'll kill you."

He gave her a quick kiss and turned to leave. "Bye, Georgia."

"I've got to go, too." Karen winked at Georgia. "I want to see you make something out of this."

"Out of what?" Wally Bishop asked, holding the door open for Karen to leave as he walked into the shop.

Karen merely smiled at Georgia and left.

"What are you up to?" Georgia asked, resting an arm on the cash register as she smiled at Wally. "You should be home preparing for the onslaught of the Columbia River Days Committee."

He leaned on the counter and smiled at her. "You coming?"

"I think as cochairperson of the committee, I'm expected to put in an appearance. And who in his right mind would ever turn down the opportunity to visit your place?"

He grinned and gestured over his shoulder toward

Ben, who was still talking with John Kirby. "You've been keeping kind of close company with Stratton lately. I thought you might have made other plans."

Georgia gave him a scolding look. "He's my landlord, Wally."

He quirked an eyebrow. "And I understand *you're his* landlady after hours."

Georgia sighed. Any hope she might have entertained that no one would notice was shot down in flames. "Who told you that?" she asked.

"It's common knowledge." He shrugged. "When the winsome widow takes a beau, news travels fast."

"He's acting as a sort of bodyguard since the break-in," she explained with a practiced ease that told him she wanted no smirks or smart remarks. In view of the way she reacted around Ben, the practiced ease was more difficult to project than she'd imagined.

Wally's expression was noncommittal. "He's letting you come alone tonight?"

"He offered to wait in the car." Georgia reached out to pat Wally's shoulder. "I assured him you'd be gentleman enough to invite him in. He's into restoring, too, you know. I'm sure he'd appreciate your home."

Wally rolled his eyes. "Soft soap, Georgia? You must really be smitten. All right, all right. Bring him along. I lost you to Gary when I was a sensitive youth. I guess I can live through losing you a second time now that I'm suave and mature." He smoothed his hair back with exaggerated affection.

Georgia laughed lightly, swatting at his arm. "You didn't love me in high school. You just wanted to date me because I was the only girl in the junior class who wasn't impressed with your Corvette." She sobered a little. "And you don't love me now. I'm part of your past, and you're in love with yesterday. That's all."

With a tolerant smile, Wally rested his eyes on Georgia. There was a pain behind them she didn't see. "So you have me all figured out?"

She shook her head. "No. I don't understand anything these days—or anyone."

He frowned at her. "Problems?"

She shrugged philosophically, coming around the counter and walking beside him as he headed toward the door. "My kids are growing up, and my own life is changing. I guess I can't help but be confused. Even my shop will look different."

Wally put an arm around her shoulders and gave them a friendly squeeze. "It'll look like it did at the turn of the century. You're as tied up with the past as I am. I'll bet it'll feel familiar to you even though you've never seen it the way it was."

That thought brought Georgia a little shudder of excitement. She did love this town. She wanted so much for it to prosper, but its heritage was rich and warm. She wanted nothing to change that. She felt a new thrill at having helped save the Jeremiah houses.

AS KIRBY SHOOK hands with Ben, then ran across the street to his truck, Ben turned toward the door of the shop. The sight of Wally Bishop with his arm around Georgia, talking intimately as they looked up the street, checked him in his tracks. What could he get for murdering a curator? he wondered. In view of his growing feelings for Georgia, Ben decided he had sufficient cause. Still, murder was a drastic measure. He could probably have the charge reduced to manslaughter when he explained his difficult childhood. Surely the district attorney would have sympathy for how much he'd missed and his fantasy that he might still have it all, which this beautiful woman had woven in his head. He lost his faculties when he looked at her or thought about her. No doubt he could plead insanity.

Ben walked toward Georgia and Wally, ready to risk murder one and the chair. Then Wally spotted him and dropped his hand from Georgia's shoulder. "Hello, Stratton. I'd like to invite you to join us at the meeting tonight."

Wondering if Bishop knew how close he'd come to an ugly demise, Ben shook his hand. "Thank you. Georgia tells me it's a turn-of-the-century showplace."

Wally smiled affably. "I'm fortunate enough to have come from a family that saved everything. See you both tonight."

"WHAT TIME should we open the beer garden?"

"Tomorrow!"

Laughter ran through the group assembled in Wally's Victorian living room.

"Traditionally, it's been seven." Georgia sent a scolding glance to Jasper Johnson, who had answered her question. She and Karen sat side by side on a horsehair and mahogany Grecian couch. Fifteen people faced them in a semicircle of antique chairs. "But the Elks would like permission to open at five this year. With the Scandinavian Society providing sausage sandwiches to go with the beer, they think they could make it a dinner event, as well. Any objections?"

A hand went up.

Ben watched the proceedings from one end of the back row of chairs. He had long ago tuned out the discussion to watch the committee and wonder if one of them could be responsible for the vandalism in Georgia's shop and the attempt to run her down. It seemed unlikely that anyone in this collection of teachers, civil servants, merchants and attorneys could be insincere about his devotion to this project or his affection for one of its cochairs. Yet it was likely that someone was.

MacKay still hadn't been found, but Ben was less and less convinced that he was responsible. Though he'd obviously been angry at Georgia, even threatened her, Ben found it hard to believe he'd have done that if he'd intended to punish her by trashing her store. Not only did it make him the obvious suspect, it blunted the effectiveness of his destruction. Ben knew his reasons weren't necessarily scientific, but he felt sure the guilty party was someone pretending to be a friend. Still…nothing had happened while MacKay had been missing.

"Tea?"

Ben came out of his thoughts with a start to find a white-haired woman holding a flute-rimmed china cup and saucer toward him. People were up and moving around, conversation buzzing. Ben reached cautiously for the cup.

"Ladyfinger?" Another woman of the same vintage offered a silver platter of delicate strips of sponge cake. He could have eaten them all, by himself, before breakfast. He took one and placed it carefully on his saucer.

"What do you think of this place?" Georgia settled into the now vacant chair beside him, a long canvas skirt covering her small-heeled shoes as she crossed her knees. She balanced an even smaller cup with yellow roses on it and three cookies on the saucer. "Doesn't it make you want to put on your starched collar and your white suit and part your hair down the middle?''

Almost ready to agree, he balked at parting his hair in the middle. "I have a cowlick," he said.

Georgia's brown eyes turned to his hair for a moment's study, then lowered to his eyes, a smile in them that robbed him of breath. "How charming of you," she said.

He hadn't seen this mood before. She was sweet and playful and just a little reckless, as though she were testing the strength of a tether with which she'd grown impatient. Suddenly feeling as if she were as strange to him as the china cup in his hand, he nibbled on the cookie. It was sweet but airy and dissolved on his tongue in an instant. He thought longingly of Linda's chocolate-chip cookies. "So where would I be going with my stiff collar, my white suit and my hair parted in the middle?''

"We give you dispensation to part it on the side," she said, glancing at him as she nibbled thoughtfully on her ladyfinger. The tip of her tongue came out to snatch a crumb off her lips, and he tried to concentrate on getting his cup to his mouth without shattering it. "Probably into some rose garden in search of your ladylove. You'd have a nosegay and chocolates.''

He smiled. "What would you be wearing?''

"Oh…'' She was off in thought again, sipping from the thin china cup. "Something white and lacy…and a wide-brimmed straw hat with a few stems of lavender in the band.'' She smiled as she continued to unravel the fantasy. "I'm a woman with plans to travel. I might become a great actress, a dancer or possibly a doctor.''

He laughed softly. "That way if you botch a surgery,

you can dance out of your patient's life and never be heard from again.''

Georgia moved her cup to her left hand and rested her right elbow on Ben's shoulder. The gesture put them eye-to-eye—hers filled with laughter, his with a kind of awe he felt but didn't understand. ''I never suspected you could be this much fun,'' she said.

''Does that mean you might change your travel plans?''

She shook her head. Her hair swung and light rippled in it. ''It means I might share the chocolates with you. Wally has invited all of us to tour the house. Would you like to?''

''Yes, of course.''

Georgia put their cups on a nearby table and led the way into the elegant parlor. Groups wandered at will, one following Wally, who explained some of the older pieces and answered questions. He fairly beamed with pride in his antique possessions. Other people took off on their own, looking around with the reverence of those fascinated by history.

But Ben had difficulty concentrating on anyone but himself—Georgia had taken his hand. ''You won't believe the kitchen,'' she said as she pulled him in that direction. He followed her, prepared to believe anything.

The kitchen was almond with dark blue accents, the tall cupboard doors bearing hand-painted illustrations of herbs and flowers. ''This is the kind of kitchen Linda should have,'' Georgia said dreamily. ''I'm sure she could become *cordon bleu* quality in this room. And under all this charm and authentic face—'' she patted the counter with its long cabinets ''—are a dishwasher, garbage disposal, microwave oven.'' She moved to an ornate cast-iron stove. ''And this beauty is wired.''

Ben grinned down at her, unable to resist the joke. ''And this beauty is wired, too, isn't she?''

She laughed, unoffended. ''This house makes me a little giddy. It's probably best that Wally got it rather than I. A few weeks in it and I'd be so steeped in Victorian atmosphere that I'd probably cease to function and become simply a decoration.''

''Oh, that wouldn't happen,'' Ben said, putting his arm around her shoulders. She wove her fingers in his as they wandered up the back stairs. ''You have to study all those medical texts between pirouettes.''

The back stairs were plain and narrow, but the pine shone. They deposited Ben and Georgia in a wide hallway that led to several guest bedrooms, a wonderful, book-lined, claret-carpeted library and what was apparently the master bedroom. Georgia stopped in the doorway. A large four-poster with ornate carvings dominated the room, its posts reaching almost to the high ceiling. A marble fireplace stood between two lace-paneled windows, and two spindly legged chairs were pulled up for conversation or dozing. Around the room were Chinese pots, silver candlesticks, paintings in gilded frames and thriving ferns.

''Wally's great-great-grandfather was a ship's captain. This house is filled with treasures from all over the world,'' Georgia said a little wistfully. ''I could never have done this with it.''

''Maybe if your ship comes in,'' Ben suggested, ''you could buy one of the other two.''

''Now that the grant came through, they belong to the museum,'' she said. ''Their protection was my primary concern. Wally plans to fill them with some of the overflow furniture from the basement of the museum. He'll do a superb job.''

To Ben, who loved restoring old buildings to their original style and elegance but preferred space and quiet lines in his private life, this was all a bit much. But Georgia loved it so much he was able to see it from a different perspective. He wasn't sure he could ever live in a place like this, but he could appreciate its warmth and cheerful clutter. As his eyes passed over the bed and settled on the chairs pulled cozily near the fireplace, an image filled his mind, unbidden, but clear.

In his stiff collar and white suit, he sat in one of the chairs looking at Georgia, who sat in the other in her white lacy dress with its rose pinned to the collar. The rose was red rather than yellow, and her hat lay discarded at the foot of the bed. Wordlessly, as though by mutual consent, they extended hands to each other and stood. He pulled off his jacket, and she began to pull the pins from her hair.

"You're getting into this, aren't you?" Georgia asked.

Ben focused on her with a little difficulty, confused by the bright scarf around her neck and the absence of a wide-brimmed hat.

"Things from the past are seductive. It's my theory that they don't want to be relegated to uselessness, so they make us see the past when we look at them. You look at an old book or a water pitcher and wonder who held it, who used it. Then, when you're really hooked, you feel that if you buy it and have it around, it'll all come to you. You'll know what the original owner thought and felt about it.'' She sighed and pulled him out of the room. He followed, his heart beating fast, his mind still disoriented.

Then he gave the chairs one last glance over his shoulder, and as he dragged his eyes away, he saw the shoes standing near the closet—and something on the sole that would have been invisible except for the soft light of the oil lamp on the table near the wardrobe.

"Wait." Suddenly alert, Ben stopped Georgia and went several steps into the room to kneel beside Wally's shoes, probably hastily changed before the meeting. He reached to the sole of the shoe and extracted a piece of straw.

"What is it?" Georgia asked, leaning over his shoulder.

Straightening, he held his palm out to her, the piece of straw picking up the light.

"What...?" She began to ask him why he'd stopped for a piece of straw. Then she remembered the piece Phil had found on the floor of her shop the morning after it had been vandalized. She shook her head. "No, no. I know what you're thinking, but that's impossible. There are lots of dishes and framed photos and stuff in the basement of the museum that are packed in straw the way they were in those days. I'm sure that's where it came from."

"That could very well be," Ben said quietly. "The question is, where did the straw in your shop come from? MacKay's or the museum basement?"

The sound of laughter and footsteps coming up the stairs captured Georgia's attention. She whispered firmly, "Wally's been helping me with this all along! He's the *curator* of the museum! He wouldn't be opposed to restoring downtown and saving two historic homes. He owns one just like them and has done wonderful things with it!" She spread her hands to indicate the beautiful room.

Ben put the piece of straw in his pocket. "Don't yell at me," he whispered back. "I can't explain it either, but this is the same stuff we found on the floor of your shop."

Georgia frowned at him, turning quickly to smile as two older ladies peered into the doorway. She pulled Ben through the bedroom's other door and into the main hallway. She backed him up against the wall and frowned again. "How can you accuse me of yelling when we're whispering?" she demanded softly.

"I know a whispered yell when I hear it," he returned. "I don't want you seeing him without me, understand? Whether it's business or pleasure."

"Don't get imperious with me!" she warned.

"How can I sound imperious," he demanded, "when I'm whispering?"

Georgia closed her eyes and drew a breath for patience. "Wally and I don't see each other socially."

"He was able to make a social occasion out of looking in on you at the shop today."

Georgia's eyes widened. "What?"

The crowd was beginning to thicken upstairs. Ben took Georgia's arm and led her down the winding main staircase. At the bottom they almost collided with Karen, who was being helped into her jacket by their host. She turned to wave at Ben and Georgia as she left, her expression speculative.

Georgia hoped she looked natural. She couldn't believe that seconds ago Ben had been suggesting that her lifelong friend might be responsible for the damage done to her shop, very nearly done to her body and very surely done to her peace of mind. Guilt that she had even listened to the suggestion made her hug Wally when he turned to her.

"This place is so wonderful, Wally. Every time I go through it, I covet it more and more."

"What did you think of the place?" Wally asked Ben.

"Very elegant and very beautiful," Ben replied sincerely. He might be suspicious of his host but not of his host's ability to recreate the warm domesticity of a fascinating period.

Georgia smiled at Wally. "I've been bragging about you all evening. Thank you for opening your home to us. The upstairs is still full of people oohing and aahing over your things."

"You run a good meeting, Georgia," Wally praised, reaching to the overburdened hall tree for the canvas jacket that matched her skirt. "We have most of the details wrapped up. Patsy Butler tells me Linda was runner-up for princess. She must be disappointed."

"Actually, she's delighted," Georgia corrected as he helped her into her jacket. Her glance bounced threateningly off Ben's watchful hazel eyes as she turned to accept Wally's help. "She's been put in charge of the high school's cookie concession, and she's thrilled to death about it. She'd rather be second prettiest, not have to make the speeches and have the opportunity to bake."

"Just like her mother," Wally said, pinching her chin. "Always happier working behind the scenes. Thanks for coming."

Wally waved them off and closed the door behind them. Georgia walked silently beside Ben to his truck and waited while he unlocked the door. Because of the fullness of her long skirt, she didn't have to wait for his help to climb into the front seat.

"Don't glower at me," Ben said from behind the

wheel as he turned the key in the ignition. "I didn't put the straw on his shoes."

Folding her arms, Georgia did glower. "What was that crack about his making a social opportunity out of visiting the shop?"

The truck roared off into the night. "He had his arm around you," Ben said calmly.

"So did you fifteen minutes ago," she reminded. "What's the difference?"

"I didn't trash your shop and almost run you down."

"Neither did he."

Ben glanced at her as he made a turn. "How do you know that for certain?"

"He's my friend!" She raised her voice impatiently. "He and Gary and Karen and Rob and I all went to school together. We palled around, double-dated. He wouldn't do that to me."

"You dated him?"

"A few times in our junior year. Then Gary and I got serious."

"How did he take being jilted for Gary?"

Georgia tried to remember so she could tell Ben he'd been a paragon of maturity. But her memories were crowded with falling in love with Gary. "He wasn't jilted," she said, her voice losing its earlier conviction. "He was very popular because he was rich and fun to be with. And he had a Corvette. He had lots of girls, and I'd only gone out with him a couple of times."

"He's still in love with you," Ben said seriously.

"He's in love with the past." Georgia turned to study his impressive profile in the shadows that raced through the truck. For a moment it distracted her. Then she remembered that she was angry with him. "You're

trying to tell me that he's done these things to me because I jilted him in high school?"

"No, I'm not. But he had straw on his shoes and
he's...a little weird about you."

"Weird about me?"

Ben sighed and shrugged. "I can't explain it."

"Because it's absurd." Georgia settled glumly into
her corner. "You're taking your role of bodyguard too
seriously."

"Good thing for you," he said. "Or you wouldn't
be here."

Annoyed because he was right, she was tired, and it
was all so unbelievable, Georgia suggested haughtily,
"Maybe it's time for you to move out."

"No."

At Ben's implacable reply, she turned to him and
reminded, "You're a *guest* in my house."

Without looking away from the road, he replied,
"And Riverfront Books is a tenant in my building—
without a lease, as I recall."

As he turned into her driveway, Georgia gaped at
him, wondering if she could have misunderstood the
suggestion that he could evict her if he so chose. The
set of his jaw convinced her that she hadn't. She accused indignantly, "That's blackmail!"

He turned the engine off, leaned back against the
upholstery and gave her an unrepentant smile. "Yeah."

Georgia looked into his eyes, now dark green in the
shadows of the truck cab, searching for the man who
only an hour ago had joined in her playful Victorian
fantasy. There was nothing of the gentle sweetness she
saw in him so often. He was dead serious and danger-
ously determined.

"How will you be able to sleep tonight?" she asked, hoping to shame him into some admission of guilt.

He laughed mirthlessly and reached his left arm out to rest his wrist on top of the steering wheel. "I haven't slept since I met you. What's one more night?"

Unsure what he meant, she said defensively, "That sofa is very comfortable."

He nodded, looking through the windshield into the night. Then he turned to her, his eyes stormy. "But my thoughts are not. I'm a little bit in love with you, Georgia."

Her anger completely derailed by that unexpected admission, she swallowed, staring at him. "Is...that possible?" she asked after a moment. "To be a little bit in love?"

He shook his head. "I don't know. I didn't think it was possible for me to fall in love at all. I've never been loved, so I've settled for being liked and respected. When I travel around to our various properties, I'm always welcomed sincerely, and since I was an orphan chucked from place to place, that's all I've ever really wanted. I've been doing fine without love. But here I am. Since I know nothing about it—except that I've never had it and don't know how to return it—I imagine I can only be a little bit in love. But it's enough to make me worry about you and be unwilling to trust anybody else with the responsibility for your safety. So humor me, will you?"

"Ben—"

"All I want to hear," he interrupted quietly, "is that you're not going to insist that I leave."

"How can I?" she demanded in exasperation. "You'd throw my bookshop out in the street. Wouldn't you?"

He considered a moment. "Possibly. I'm at least as stubborn as you are."

Georgia folded her arms and leaned back against the door. "If you stay, I won't have you making cracks about Wally."

He nodded. "I'll keep my opinions to myself."

"And I'd be careful about telling me who I can and cannot see and when."

"I don't care who you see or when," he said, "as long as I'm with you. I promised Bea I'd keep an eye on you." He inspected the fingernails on his free hand. "I suppose she could make your life difficult if you make my job difficult."

"You're very unscrupulous."

He shrugged modestly. "I've been blessed."

Suddenly very tired, she paused a moment to contemplate the long drop to the pavement. Climbing up without assistance had been one thing, vaulting down was another. Ben came around the truck to stand in front of her. "Need a hand?" he asked, smiling.

She peered down. "That, or rappeling gear." Thinking he intended to offer her his hand, Georgia extended hers. Instead, he put an arm around her back, the other under her knees, and lifted her out. "Close the door, will you please?" he asked, turning her so that she could reach it. Flustered, excited, charmed, she complied.

Looping her arms around his neck, Georgia relaxed for the brief walk to the back door. "This is probably beyond the call of your duties," she said, her heart ticking against her ribs with a strong steadiness she suspected he could feel against his chest.

He dipped under her spirea bush, then turned sideways through the gate that connected the edge of the house to the workshop. "This has nothing to do with my duties," he said quietly.

"What does it have to do with?"

"A sudden need to have my arms filled with you." The still dormant climbing roses woven in the trellis that covered the patio rustled in the night breeze. Lilac and camellia perfumed the air.

Is this really happening to me? Georgia wondered. She had only to tighten her arms to assure herself that it was. There were sturdy shoulders under her hands, strong arms supporting her, wiry hair that smelled of a man's shampoo only inches from her nose. Awareness rose in her, demanding her attention. It was the wrong time, and probably the wrong man, but something deep inside her didn't seem to care. "Because you're a little bit in love with me."

They had reached the door and he stopped, still carrying her. He looked into her eyes and nodded as though that admission disturbed as well as pleased him. "Yes."

With a small sigh, Georgia leaned her forehead against his. "This is going to be a problem for us."

He nuzzled her face aside to plant a light kiss near her ear. "It's my problem," he said. "It doesn't have to affect you. I understand the limitations of my job."

She sighed again and pulled back slightly to look into his eyes. They were dark in the shadows. "I'd like to make it that easy for you, but I can't."

He studied her a moment. "I take exception to the word 'easy,' but what do you mean?"

"I'm a little bit in love with you," she said. "So it will affect me, and I think that confuses the limitations of your job."

He seemed to be smiling and frowning at the same

time, or maybe it was a trick of the shadows. "But you were snapping at me a minute ago."

"You threatened to evict me."

He laughed throatily. "I have a unique approach to courting." He sobered suddenly and leaned down to set her on her feet. Then he took a firm grip on her shoulders and looked into her eyes. "I don't know what to do about this. I...I..." Almost daily he made decisions involving large amounts of money and people's jobs, and here he was stammering.

"I know," Georgia said quietly, remembering what he'd told her about never having had love and being unable to give it. "I'm not ready for this, either. Yet, here we are. The important thing is not to panic. This could all be a reaction to the strange circumstances. You're attracted to the damsel in distress, and I'm idolizing the storybook hero. Maybe it'll go away."

He doubted that seriously. It wasn't a troublesome itch, it was a need—almost a pain deep in his gut. He couldn't see it conveniently disappearing. "That's wishful thinking, Georgia."

"Well then, you tell me how to handle it," she said with sudden impatience. "The last time I was in love I was seventeen. I'm not a practiced hand at this."

A little surprised but also pleased by that little slip of control, Ben reminded her gently, "I thought you said the important thing was not to panic."

She tried to shake his hands off. "Well, I've changed my mind. I mean, I have two kids to think of, and Gary's...Gary's..."

He understood her love for Gary—his own respect and admiration for the man grew the longer he occupied his shop—but at the moment, he didn't want to hear about him. Retaining his hold on Georgia, he pulled her closer and stopped her worried ramblings with his lips.

Her sigh of frustration then acceptance filled his mouth. Her lips responded to his with the same eagerness and urgency he felt; her tongue toyed with his without constraint. He felt her light weight incline against him as she tried to accommodate his height. The roaming of her small hands across his back, up the sensitive ridge of his spine, up and down his sides made putty of his determination to retain control of this kiss.

Georgia felt the subtle change in his touch and his stance. She'd been held and kissed enough times to know surrender when she felt it. A part of her that wasn't occupied with delight and sensation thought how ironic that was; she'd thought she was the one surrendering. Could it be that a true battle of the sexes involved only mutual surrender and no conqueror? It was too complex a thought for a mind lost to the demands of her body.

Ben's hands were everywhere and she was too occupied with the sensations they were causing to give any thought to stopping him. Her back and shoulders were a mass of tremors, her breasts felt swollen against the armor plate of his chest, and the hips that had taken one light, brief pass of his hands wanted more. She was all nerve endings and pounding heart. She had no breath at all.

They emerged from the kiss, gasping and leaning on each other. "I'm...glad we're just a little bit in love," Georgia whispered, her voice strangled. "I don't think I could live through a grand passion."

Ben straightened and drew a ragged breath. "This could be a bigger problem than we first imagined.

You'd better get inside.'' He pulled the screen door open while she routed blindly in her purse for her keys. When she found them and pushed the door open, he put an arm up across the door frame to block her way. She looked up in the light filtering out from the kitchen and saw a wry smile on his face. ''It also occurs to me that the rewards could be bigger.'' He leaned down to kiss her lightly, then turned and headed for the workshop. She flipped on the porch light to guide him, and he turned back with a wave, his smile still in place. Georgia closed the door and leaned against it for a moment, trying desperately to collect her fragmented thoughts. They refused to come. Feeling was still so strong in her heart and throughout her body that she could not recall or analyze or predict. She could only tremble and smile and know she was in trouble.

Her smile widened as one thought did take shape. Ben was in trouble, too.

CHAPTER EIGHT

DRESSED IN BATHROBE and cat-faced slippers, Georgia wandered groggily down to the kitchen, intent on putting the coffee on. Ben had been faithfully fixing breakfast for a week, but it was only 5:00 a.m. Even he wouldn't be stirring for another hour. Since sleep insisted on eluding her, she sought to thwart it completely with a jolt of caffeine. Midnight meowed at her from his comfortable perch on one of the chairs.

The shrill ring of the telephone startled her, and she scuffed toward it, frowning. "Hello?" she said.

"Georgia?"

At the shaky sound of Karen's voice, she came fully alert, afraid of what she was about to hear. "Yes, Karen. What's wrong?"

There was a small sob and Georgia's stomach tightened. "Phil's been shot!" There was another sob and Georgia unconsciously put a hand over her eyes, waiting for more. "He's all right, sort of. I mean, it was just in the leg, but I...I'm a mess."

"Where are you?"

"At Columbia Memorial."

"I'll be right there." Control asserted itself and Georgia's brain began to work. "Give me ten minutes."

In her I-function-best-in-a-crisis mode, she wasn't even surprised when Ben stepped out of the service porch, a wrench in his hand, a frown between his eyes. "What is it?" he asked.

She hung up the phone and began tearing off her robe as she headed for the stairs. "Phil's been shot," she explained over her shoulder. "Karen's at the hospital."

"I'll get my keys," he shouted up the stairs, "and wait for you in the truck."

In five minutes she was in jeans and a sweatshirt bending over Linda and shaking her lightly.

"Mmmf?" Linda asked, opening one eye, which seemed to refuse to focus.

"Honey, Mr. Hansen's had an accident and I'm going to the hospital. Can you get yourself and Lacey going in time for school if I don't get back?"

Linda propped up on an elbow, rubbing a hand over her eyes. "What happened? Is he okay?"

"I think so. I don't really know the details." Georgia kissed her forehead, pushed her back against the pillow and pulled the covers over her. "If you get a chance to call me between classes, I'll probably be able to tell you more. I've got to go."

Ben's Le Mans-style drive to the hospital had Georgia running through the emergency room doors eleven minutes after she'd hung up the telephone. Karen ran into her arms, sobbing, "I knew this would happen! Didn't I tell you this would happen?"

"How is he?" Ben asked, leading both women to the beige vinyl waiting room sofa.

Karen glanced up at him broodingly, her eyes red from crying, her cheeks puffy and blotched. "It's just a flesh wound. He's going to be fine, then I'm going to kill him."